PUDSEY
THE DOG
MOVIE

PUDSEY
THE DOG
MOVIE

LITTLE, BROWN BOOKS FOR YOUNG READERS
www.lbkids.co.uk

LITTLE, BROWN BOOKS FOR YOUNG READERS

First published in Great Britain in 2014 by Little, Brown Books for Young Readers
Reprinted 2014 (twice)

Copyright © Simco Limited, 2014
With special thanks to Catherine Coe

A CIP catalogue record for this book
is available from the British Library.

ISBN 978-0-349-12427-8

Typeset in Minion by M Rules
Printed and bound in Great Britain by
Clays Ltd, St Ives plc

Papers used by LBYR are from well-managed forests
and other responsible sources.

MIX
Paper from
responsible sources
FSC
www.fsc.org   FSC® C104740

Little, Brown Books for Young Readers
An imprint of
Little, Brown Book Group
100 Victoria Embankment
London EC4Y 0DY

An Hachette UK Company
www.hachette.co.uk

www.lbkids.co.uk

CHAPTER ONE

This is it! I thought as I sat on a silk-covered chaise longue. I was staring into the camera on a 1930s film set. *This is what I've been waiting for my whole life. My screen debut!*

I'd spent an hour in doggy make-up, which included a lavender conditioning bath (yuk!) and a guaranteed 'super-silky-smooth' blow dry. According to my stylist, Jacintha, this was guaranteed to give me the glossiest coat ever. I'd had my nose rubbed with essential oils and hairs combed and fluffed in places I never even knew I had hairs. But it was all worth it, right?

"Let's stand by to shoot, everyone," said a voice from the shadows. "Here we go. *The Artistic*, forty-eight, take one."

But wouldn't you know it? Straight away, the leading lady and leading man stepped in my limelight. They completely blocked the camera's view of me as they talked in drawling American accents. *Blah, blah, blah, blah, blah.* (A runner on set had told me their names but my memory's never been that great. Apparently, they were famous. All I knew was that neither of them had given me a single treat. In fact, they'd barely looked at me. It was very disappointing.)

I looked up at the white-haired director and the crowd of film people behind him, hoping for a signal for me to platform one of my many talents – to spin a pirouette, perform a crouch 'n' roll, or at least wag my tail. I had a very attractive tail, after all, especially after this morning's grooming. But no one so much as looked at me.

This is so boring, I thought. *My first movie, and the director has me sitting here like a rug!* This should have been the start of something big. Where was my moment in the spotlight?

"And action!" called the director.

The leading lady sat down next to me. Maybe she was going to hold her hands out to indicate I should perform a roll, or lean forward so I could leap over her back. *Ta-da!* But, instead, she just looked up at the leading man with big gleaming eyes.

"I'm telling ya, kid – the talkie is dead. Smellovision is the future," he said.

"Smello-what?" The lady raised her eyebrows.

"Vision," the man explained. "Imagine if you could actually smell what you saw on a movie screen. Expensive perfume. Delicious roast chicken. Dirty dog breath."

The leading lady screwed up her face. "Yeesh!"

Oi, I thought. There was nothing wrong with my

3

breath. I cleaned with Dog-Mint Dentals every day!

The leading man drawled on. "Why, we'll stink up every movie theatre from here to Wisconsin."

"Oh ... but come on, you said I had a shot at *Gone with the Wind*." What *was* she talking about? What wind? It wasn't me, and I hoped the director knew that – there's nothing worse than a dog who can't control his bodily urges!

The lady stood up from the sofa and put her hand on the man's arm. The camera swivelled to face them. Now I wasn't even in shot!

"That turkey? Forget about it!" he said, shaking his head.

Oh, enough of this nonsense! Time to liven things up, I thought. *Wait till they see what I can really do.* I jumped to the floor and stood upright on my hind legs. With my paws in the dancing position, my tail raised – with a slight curl for maximum cuteness – I turned in a circle. "Ba, be, ba, be, baba," I hummed as I moonwalked towards the actors. The leading lady looked down at me – ha, I had her attention now. "They're loving this!" I said to myself, giving a double pirouette – perfectly, in my opinion.

"What is that mutt doing?" hissed the director, who sat in his fold-up chair while his assistants brought him cups of tea and scribbled down notes of everything he said. "Cut, cut!"

Ooops, better scarper! I dropped to all fours as one of the assistants chased me off the stage.

"Pudsey, get out of there!"

As I raced away, through the legs of the leading man, I heard a tearing noise, then a crash, a bang, a *BOOM*. I turned around, and saw that he'd fallen into the leading lady, who had fallen into a camera man who had crashed into a set ladder. The set came crashing down all around me! I lay down in the 'take cover' position and covered my eyes, but allowed myself a peek from behind my paw ... The white gazebo standing above the director wobbled back and forth precariously. The director scrambled out from under it just as it toppled down in one big tent-pole mess.

"CUT!" screamed the director, his white hair flopping about like a fluttering dove. "YOU'RE FIRED!" He jabbed his finger at me, his ugly face turning puce with anger.

I lifted my head in astonishment. *What did I do?*

"Get that dog out of here. You'll never work in this town again." The director slumped back in his chair. "Where's the stand-in dog? Get him here."

Now, I'm not stupid – I know when I'm not wanted, although I had a good mind to tell the nose-in-the-air, snooty Jack Russell who ran on to the set past me just what he was letting himself in for. The leading lady began rubbing his neck and fussing over him. She'd never made a fuss of me like that! *Ah, I'm better off on my own.* I thought. *Anyway, you know what they say, as one door closes, another one always opens.*

I ran from the stale air of the film studio and into the bright sunshine outside, past the costume trailer and make-up van. It felt good to be moving around again after being perched on that chaise longue for so long. I felt sorry for the Jack Russell, no matter how stuck up he was. I was certain he would soon be bored out of his mind. (Although, as every dog knows, Jack Russells have tiny brains. So maybe severe boredom wouldn't be a problem for him!)

I looked at the film crew rushing about outside, their hair frazzled, faces pulled into frowns, pointing in different directions and shouting into mobile phones. My stomach rumbled, and I stopped to think for a moment ... now I was no longer required, I could focus on the things that made me most happy. *Food!* But I could tell with one sniff there wasn't a sausage anywhere near this set. *Exploring* – yes, that

7

was a better idea . . . and I could search for something to fill my empty belly at the same time.

"What's that dog doing out here?" someone yelled as I rounded the corner of a trailer.

Uh-oh! I had to get far away from here – fast!

CHAPTER TWO

I love the Tube. Whizzing past stations quicker than I could ever run no matter how many rashes of bacon I'd had for breakfast that morning. I waited next to the doors as the train rumbled along. I was sat between a sleeping toddler in a pram and a man whose red trousers flapped around his ankles. I sniffed at them, wondering if they'd shrunk in the wash.

A women in a fake-fur coat (at least I hoped it was fake) kept staring at me and frowning. *What?! Have you never seen a dog riding the Tube before?* I thought to myself.

The train began to slow and I held a paw out to the rail to balance myself as the carriage shuddered to a stop. The sliding doors *pinged* and then *swooshed* open and I ran out into the yellow-tiled underground station, up the steps, jogging up the escalator and finally diving under the ticket gates (being a small dog has its benefits). I could smell it now: the smell of freedom, of a day doing whatever I wanted, of eating what I wanted, of exploring, chasing, having fun. One last set of stairs took me past tourists pouring down into the station, as I emerged outside into the welcoming smog of London. I looked at the weird-looking winged-man statue that rose up from the top of a huge fountain. Here I was – Piccadilly Circus!

Lights flashed all around – from cameras hung around people's necks, from the giant digital billboards covering the buildings, from the headlights of the buses and black cabs which sped around the busy junction. I took in the sounds as I weaved through legs and bicycles and buggy wheels – the chattering of humans, engines roaring, car horns beeping, the strums of a busker with a guitar. The busker wore a sparkling blue sequined suit, and was playing 'Don't Worry, Be Happy'. I broke out into a dance as he sang. He grinned and pirouetted with me. *Wow*, I thought, *this is much more fun than a film set!*

"I like you!" the busker said when more and more people dropped handfuls of coins into his upturned hat. But, as much as I was having fun, I couldn't hang around with him all day. And, would you believe it, not one person dropped a doggy treat into the hat instead of coins! I needed to find some food – and maybe see the sights at the same time ... A bus stopped in front of us, with 'The Big Bus Tour of London' splashed across its side. Perfect! I waved a paw to the busker, leapt through the doors and ran up to the top deck – to the front seat. *Woo hoo!*

"Don't worry, be happy," I sang as the bus drove

along. I didn't know the rest of the lyrics, but that didn't matter – I like to make my own ones up anyway. "In my life I can do what I want, no one to bother me, no one to stop my fun. Oh, don't worry, be happy!"

The ivory turrets of the Tower of London soon loomed up in front of me and I rushed back down the bus staircase. As I waited for the bus to slow down at the next stop, a baby in a buggy next to me dangled a biscuit right in my nose. *That's kind!* I thought, but just as I opened my mouth to snaffle it the mum swiped it away. "Joshua, that's for you, not to feed to flea-ridden dogs!" she hissed.

Huh – how rude! I take my flea treatments very seriously – no self-respecting acting-dog can afford to risk infecting a movie set.

Outside the Tower, I inspected the big men in great red suits with black trims who stood guard in front of the Tower. "They look funny," I said to myself, "a bit like chubby clowns!" But their faces weren't smiley. Their mouths were set in a straight line, eyes serious. I thought I should put on my best impersonation of a human if I was going to get inside the tower for a closer look. Maybe there was a kitchen in there with some roast chicken! *Mmmmmm, roast chicken.* My mouth was already watering.

I stood up on my hind legs and walked over to two of the men beside an archway.

"Eh, Billy, have you ever seen this before?" said one of them, nudging the other. "A standing dog!"

He reached down to pat my head, but I ducked away quickly. *How patronising!* Standing was the least of my abilities. Fortunately, they stepped aside to let me in anyway, and I ran around the castle, checking out all the different towers and Traitor's Gate. I jumped up to read the signs for visitors – some of the history stuff was really interesting. For instance, did you know that Traitor's Gate was where prisoners were taken into the tower – by boat from the Thames? *Awesome!* But there wasn't a single whiff of a chicken being roasted. Time to keep going!

Back outside the Tower, I spotted a crisp packet being blown about in the breeze. Excellent – I was sure there'd be some crumbs to ward off my hunger. But just as I ran up to it, two waddling pigeons got there first, pulling either side of the packet with their beaks. Argh – why wasn't getting food ever simple? It wasn't all bad though – chasing was my favourite thing, after eating, of course! And pigeons were perfect for that, with their wobbly bottoms and weak little wings.

"Oi, mate, what d'ya fink yer doing?" one particularly chubby pigeon squawked at me.

"Givvus a break! This is pigeon territory!" squealed a grey pigeon as it hopped around on a bench.

"I'm coming to get you!" I shouted, scampering about in circles, making the pigeons flap up and down, up and down. *Now this really is the best day ever!* I thought. Then my stomach growled, reminding me that the day would be even better with some food in my belly.

Luckily, one of those 'Big Bus Tour' red buses drew to a stop in front of the tower. I hopped on board and went to sit on the top deck, front seat, of course. I'd have a great view from here of all the restaurants in London. I could take my pick! I let my fur ruffle in the breeze for a moment, tipping my head back and closing my eyes. Oh, how brilliant it was that I could please myself and do what I wanted – I had no one else to worry about! When I opened my eyes I saw the Great British flag fluttering on a pole from a large white building. Buckingham Palace! That's what I'd visit next, home of the Queen of England. Who knew, maybe she'd even invite me in for tea! I'd always fancied trying cucumber sandwiches.

But when I padded up to the gates, the royal guards in their funny tall fluffy hats didn't move to open them – they certainly didn't seem as friendly as the guards at the Tower of London. *Hhhmmm, what to do?* Tourists crowded around the railings, so I pushed my nose under the iron bars, hoping to squeeze beneath them when the guards weren't looking. But I couldn't fit through, no matter how much I squashed my head to the ground.

There was nothing else for it. Time to use my best routine! I got up on my hind legs, paws aloft, and did an extra special quick-step pirouette dance for the guards and the Queen. It was a routine I'd been practising for months. I hoped the Queen was watching through one of the high windows and she'd order the guards to let me in. I thought I saw them smiling and laughing under their giant furry hats, but after the whole exhausting routine they just shook their heads at me. OK, so it was time to give up.

Where to next?

I followed my nose, which I could always rely on to

seek out the tastiest food nearby, and wandered along the streets of London. I held my snout up, sniffing the air, and I was soon rewarded – sweet, smoky, sour smells floated towards me. I looked around ... I was in a strange, rather exotic part of town, where red lanterns hung between the streets and rows of golden cat ornaments waved from windows. But all I really cared about were the delicious spicy smells wafting out of every single door.

A sign on the wall said: 'Welcome to Chinatown'. *Hhhhmmm.* I'd never had Chinese food before. But if it smelt this good, it *had* to be tasty.

"Hey, fluffball, you'll get into trouble if you go in there," hissed a skinny tabby cat curled up at a doorway. "Don't you dare try to steal my scraps!"

Trouble? Not me. I could be in and out of a kitchen without so much as a mouse noticing. I squeezed through the gap in the doorway and hurtled along a corridor, down some narrow steps and into a red-tiled kitchen filled with the noise of pans clinking and food sizzling. A plate of sticky ribs nestled on the counter. My mouth watered and my eyes glazed over. Those ribs had 'Pudsey' written all over them. In one fluid motion I jumped up, pawed the ribs off the plate, cradled them in my mouth and shot back out of the kitchen. As quick as lightning – I was sure no one saw me.

"Hey! What's that mutt doing in here? He's got the ribs!"

Uh-oh, so maybe an eagle-eyed chef *had* noticed. It was time to scarper.

"Out of my way!" I screamed at the lazy cat still sprawled in the doorway, ribs flying out of my mouth. I felt the waiter grab at my tail as I leapt out into the street, relieved to see a group of tourists right outside. The crowd was just perfect for losing an angry chef.

"Get him – get that dog!" yelled the man, but I quickly wove around the tourists' legs. I risked a look back at the chef. He was trying to shove his way through the crowd. Of course, he had no idea that being chased was my third favourite thing after eating and chasing pigeons. 'Can't catch me!' I cried, as I sprinted down the nearest alley. He'd have to run fast to catch Pudsey!

CHAPTER THREE

Blimey, I thought. *He was persistent* ... I huffed and puffed across yet another junction. The chef at my local pie shop only ever chased me as far as the street corner before giving up. But this person was still running. I cast another glance back and ... *phew!* It finally looked as if he'd had enough.

I turned another corner, just to be sure I'd lost him. The street looked familiar. *Oooh, is that Abbey Road?* The white stripes of the infamous zebra crossing were impossible to miss. Do you know the ones? The Beatles had been photographed walking across this street for one of their record covers – my favourite of all of their albums, too. *I wonder if I can look just as good as them?* I thought.

I stood up straight on my hind legs and began to cross the zebra crossing. At each stripe I stopped and posed, imagining the cameras clicking in front of me. You never know, maybe a director would come past right at this moment, spot me and demand I feature in his next music video. *Work it, baby, yes, work it!*

Screech! I jumped as a white van missed my tail by millimetres, swerving across the road. I gave a growl. I bet The Beatles had never had to worry about being run over. I scampered on to the pavement, shaking. That had been quite a scare for a little dog like me.

With my heart thumping like a hammer in my chest, I knew I needed to find my Zen place, to calm down a bit. I was in luck – as I turned the corner a huge park came into view. *Ah, a nice walk in peace should do it.*

I ran through the open gates (phew, no guards to worry about!) and across the grass, around trees and hedges, chasing the odd squirrel (although admittedly they weren't half as much fun as pigeons, since they ran up trees to hide all the time). *This is great*, I thought. *Best day ever. On my own with no one to bother me.*

As I rounded a hedge I spotted a mum, dad and their daughter sitting on a picnic blanket, throwing a stick to their black Labrador puppy. "Ooh, what's going on over there?" I lay down and watched the family. It was nice to see such smiling, relaxed humans, away from the craziness of the London streets. I tipped my head to one side, wondering if they'd ask me to join in. But they looked like they were having too much fun to notice me. I felt my heart sink to my paws.

Pudsey, what are you doing? I asked myself. I stood up and gave myself a good shake. I'd been stupid to think I wanted to join in with their silly games! "Who needs families? Not me. No way. I'm just going to hang out here, thinking about how much ... Oh, look, a Boris bus! I've never been on one of those. It's time to quit this joint!"

I left the family and chased towards the shiny red Boris bus that had stopped outside the park gates. "Wait. Wait for me!" The back of the brand-new bus gleamed in the sunshine and I leapt on to the open platform just as it was pulling off. (Did I mention I do dog gymnastics as well as acting? No need for a stunt double with me!)

I ran upstairs and looked around for a space on the top deck. *Oh, wow, a back seat – brilliant!* I settled down on it. I had a feeling this bus would take me somewhere special – maybe even to a sausage factory, if I was lucky! I kept my eyes peeled and my nose near the open window, but my attention was quickly taken by the kids who sat in front of me. They all wore the same grey and yellow uniform (very unflattering!). Three of them sat on the right side of the bus, three on the left. The two groups didn't look like friends. On the right were two girls and a boy with a shaved head, and they were giggling and whispering. The girl and two younger boys on the left were quiet – the girl was putting on make-up and one of the boys had his eyes glued to the screen of a games console. The smallest boy, with black shaggy hair, just stared out of the window. *I know how he feels*, I thought. *He's probably starving and looking for some tasty grub, too.*

The boy on the right suddenly got up and knelt backwards on the seat in front of the make-up girl. "Hey, it's Molly, right?" he said. "I've noticed you at school."

"Really?" Molly looked up, her eyebrows raised. "Yeah, I've seen you too."

"Cool. Listen, do you wanna go out sometime?"

"Are you actually asking me out?" Molly asked.

Ah, young love. I thought. *Bleugh!*

The boy screwed up his face and shook his head. "Nah, can't do it!"

I stared at the shaven-headed boy – so he hadn't been serious? It was just a dare? That was a bit mean!

"Hey, man," shouted the boy behind Molly, clearly trying to stick up for her. Although she didn't seem too bothered. Or perhaps she was used to it.

"Don't worry about it, George," she said, looking over at the laughing bullies. "Sticks and stones will break my bones, but words—" She broke off as a drinks cup flew across the bus and hit her smack on the forehead. The bullies' giggles grew louder as Molly turned her head away.

I let out a low growl. That was out of order. Why didn't they just leave her alone?!

I was glad when the bus slowed down for the next stop. Molly, George and the shaggy-haired boy raced down the stairs, and I found myself following them. I don't really know why, I guess I just wanted to make sure these kids were OK. What can I tell you? I'm a softy at heart! When I jumped off the last step on to the pavement I noticed the three bullies getting off too, from the front doors of the bus.

"Oi, freak, aren't you going to give him a goodbye kiss?" This was one of the bully-girls, who had rounded on Molly, stepping into her path.

"Hey, we all know my sister's a massive weirdo," said George, coming up to Molly's side, "but she's *our* massive weirdo, so get lost."

Uh-oh. I sensed this was about to get messy.

The bully-boy walked up to the shaggy-haired boy, towering over him. "Got something to say, shrimpoid?"

Wow, I thought. These bullies were nasty pieces of work – and not even brave enough to pick on kids their own size. I paced up and down at a distance, watching anxiously.

"Tommy doesn't talk," interrupted Molly.

"Oh yeah, what's wrong with him?"

"Nothing. He just doesn't talk." Molly pushed her face right into bully-boy's. I stopped pacing and let out a yip of delight. *Go, Molly!*

"So back off!" added George, shoving both hands into bully-boy's side.

"Or what!" bully-boy asked, his fists clenching.

George swung into a martial arts pose, his left arm curled above him, his right arm pointing out in front. "I'm a master at Feng Shui."

Wait – that's about balancing rooms, isn't it? I thought. Not an ancient art of defence . . .

I winced as bully-boy reached out towards George. "Wait, no, please don't. Please don't!" George yelled. The bully grabbed the back of George's underpants and wrenched them up and over his head, the red-and-blue checked pattern stretching at the seams. "Ow, ow ow ow!" George squeaked, jumping up and down in pain. *That's got to hurt!*

Something fizzed inside of me. The bullies needed more of a match. *I'm going to regret this*, I thought as I ran towards the group. Still, I sprang up and lunged at bully-boy. (I might be small, but I'm also surprisingly mighty.) My paws flying into his chest knocked him off-balance and he fell to the floor with a yelp.

"Leave them alone!" I barked. "I hate bullies." The bully-kids began walking away at last. *Good riddance!*

I looked up at Molly, who reached out a hand and gave my ears a stroke. I'm not too proud to admit that it felt good. "What a brave dog," she said with a smile.

"How come he gets all the credit?" said George, his arms flailing about as he tried to yank his pants back over his head.

"Ask me again when you're not talking to me from the inside of your underpants." Molly winked as she finally released George from the pant-misery. "So, do you think he's a stray?"

"Smells like one," replied George. *Huh – the cheek!*

He bent down and pulled gently at the name badge on my collar. "There's no address – it just says 'Pudsey.'"

"We should at least give him something to say thank you," said Molly.

My ears pricked up. *Great idea!*

"I think we've got some sausages at home ..."

Sausages? Mmmmm, sausages ... Well, what are we waiting for? I thought. *Lead the way, my lady!*

CHAPTER FOUR

I jumped up the porch steps and followed the kids through their front door. Large cardboard boxes were piled up everywhere, lining the hallway – some closed, some open with newspaper spilling out. They all had different words scrawled on them: 'living room', 'Molly's bedroom', 'stuff for loft'.

What's going on in here? I wondered, looking around at the chaos. *It's messier than a kitten-litter tray!* Maybe the family had just moved in – or were about to move out?

I followed the kids into the kitchen, which was also full of boxes. A red-headed lady stood there, staring into an open cupboard. "Hi, kids," she said, without looking round. "How was school?"

"Fine," said George as he pulled out the games console from his rucksack.

"Um, Mum ... " began Molly, sitting down at the kitchen table. I leapt up beside her. Where were the sausages?

"What?" asked the lady. She turned round and saw me for the first time. Her eyes immediately boggled. "What's a dog doing at my kitchen table?! Where did it come from?"

It?! I'm a real animal, you know – and a he!

"That's what I was about to tell you," explained Molly, giving me another stroke.

"We found him on the street," said George without looking up. He tapped at the console keys. "Can he stay with us?"

"We checked his collar," Molly added, "and his name's Pudsey. But there's no address or phone number."

The lady shook her head. "Don't be ridiculous – we're not keeping him," she sighed.

What? I thought I'd just been coming here for sausages. Not to be kept*!*

"But, Mum . . ." groaned Molly and George.

"I'm sorry, guys, but between moving house and a new job, I've just got too much on my plate already." She began hurriedly wrapping mugs in newspaper then packing them into a box on the worktop. Ah, so the family were moving *out*.

I tilted my head, putting on my best 'I'm so funny and friendly you can't resist me' face. I may not have necessarily wanted to be 'kept', but as any true actor would admit, I also hated rejection. And who could resist this face?

"But it's just not fair," argued Molly, her elbows on

the table, head in her hands. "We're moving to the countryside, not a flat."

Their mum turned briefly to look the kids straight in the eye. "The landlord said clearly: no dogs."

Thanks a lot, I thought. *There's nothing wrong with dogs, especially well-behaved ones like me.* Not that I particularly wanted to go to the countryside, but that was beside the point. Although it seemed as if these kids could do with some protecting, and perhaps I was the best dog for the job – that's if I ever wanted to live with a family, of course!

"But it sucks enough that we're moving to some stupid cottage with no WiFi," said George, still staring at his games console. "Can't we at least have a pet?"

His mum's face turned stern. She reached over and grabbed the console out of George's hands.

"No way!" he yelled. "My baby!"

"You are too attached to your games," said his

mum, already back at the cupboard and packing the console into a box.

"That's because they're awesome," George explained.

I rested my head on the table. The argument was becoming a bit boring. I wanted to know where this food was that I'd been promised. "Anyone?" I barked, looking around for the smallest sign of a titbit. "I'm still here." But they took no notice whatsoever – they clearly had their own problems, never mind little ol' me.

"You spend far too much time staring at screens." Their mum picked up a trophy and passed it to Tommy, who stared into one of the open boxes in the hallway. "Tommy, can you pop that in Daddy's box, please, love." Tommy took the trophy but still said nothing.

George looked over at his brother. "You wouldn't complain if I spent my life staring at a tree."

"No, I'd send you to a psychologist," replied his mum.

Molly giggled, then turned to Tommy. I followed her gaze. He was fingering an old watch in the box. It must have been his dad's. While his mum wasn't looking, I saw Tommy pluck it out and pop it in his pocket. His big brown eyes were turned down, dull and lifeless. *Aww, why does he look so sad?* I wondered.

"What if we got a goldfish?" their mum suggested, continuing to pull things out of cupboards and into boxes.

"Goldfish are rubbish," groaned George.

"It's basically like having a pet glove," Molly joked.

"Yeah," George agreed. I have to admit, I did too — and goldfish weren't only boring, they were rude to anyone who so much as took a slurp from their tank water. As if they didn't have enough to share around!

Molly got up, took a glass from the worktop and

opened the fridge. She yanked the door open and . . .
BULLSEYE! *Sausages! A whole plate of juicy
Lincolnshires by the looks of it!* I needed to get someone's attention and remind them of the treat I'd been
promised. I jumped down from the table, skittered
across the kitchen tiles and stretched up on my rear
legs, ready to perform.

This has to be worth at least one sausage, I thought
as I tiptoed from foot to foot. *Or ten, maybe?* "Look –
I'm walking, like a human!"

The family all stopped what they were doing and
stared at me as I turned in a circle, paws aloft. "Ha, ha,
ha! Check it out, guys!"

Molly was so distracted, she forgot about the milk
she'd been pouring and it overflowed from the glass.

"Eugh, milk's for cats!" I cried as it splashed all over
the floor – and me.

"Look how clever he is! Now can we keep him?"
pleaded George, his eyes wide as Molly knelt down to

wipe the milk from the floor. "We could enter him for shows and stuff!"

Their mum took the milk bottle, put it back in the fridge, and slammed the door. "NO. This is supposed to be a fresh start, just the four of us." Her eyes were red-rimmed and squinty – like she'd been doing a lot of crying lately, and some more tears might just pop out any second. "But I promise that before we go, we'll find Pudsey a good home." She glanced over at me, smiling kindly. "Won't we, boy?"

George sagged his head down, defeated. I dropped to all fours and groaned. *Still no sausages!*

CHAPTER FIVE

My stomach was growling like a Rottweiler as we stood outside a strange, new house. Molly rang the doorbell. *I hope this place has something to eat!* I thought. Even a slice of Spam would do.

An older lady answered the door. She was dressed head to toe in eye-squinting pink. *Eurgh!* I hated the colour pink more than anything else. "Hello, my dears," she said in a sing-song voice. She looked down at me and rubbed her hands together in glee. "This must be *Pudsey*." I really didn't like the way she said my name and had to resist the urge to whine.

"Thanks for doing this, Mrs Willoughby," said Molly.

"Oh, there's always room for another one," she replied with a grin.

I wondered what was going on – Molly, George and Tommy all had their mouths turned down. George had his hands shoved deep in his pockets, and Molly held an arm around Tommy.

"You will look after him, won't you?" asked George. Look after me? I didn't like the sound of that.

"He's kind of special," added Molly.

Yeah, I thought, *'special' is my middle name.* These kids learned fast!

Mrs Willoughby towered over me, like a very unattractive, pink skyscraper. *Double eurgh!* "Oh, I can see that," she agreed, still rubbing her hands together. Dozens of golden bracelets rattled on her arms. Then she pursed her lips and started making a weird kissing noise. Was she trying to tell me she had food?

"Got any sausages? I'm starving," I barked, looking up at her with my big doggy eyes. I was so hungry, I didn't care who fed me, as long as it was *soon*!

But she didn't get the message at all – just straightened up and turned back to the kids. "Good luck with the new start," she said, briskly. It was almost as though she wanted them to leave as soon as possible. "Come on, Pudsey," she warbled.

"OK, where's the kitchen?" I asked, rushing inside the house, chasing the siren call of sausages. "Out the back, this way? Come on!"

The door slammed on Molly, Tommy and George, but I was already busy exploring the house, looking for those elusive sausages. Mrs Willoughby was right behind me. "Now, you are going to have the best time ever here, Pudseypoos."

Pudseypoos? That's not my name! I looked into the first door that led from the hall and jumped back in shock. The entire room was decorated in pink and lace – pink curtains, pink carpet, pink flowery wall-paper. There were cream lace nets, lace tablecloths and lace doilies. It was the most badly decorated room I had ever seen (not that I'd seen a whole lot of them – I'm not the kind of dog who just wanders into strangers' houses), and it looked as if it hadn't been touched since the seventies!

"Let me introduce you to the others," said Mrs W. She pushed the door further open and I gasped in horror.

You've got to be joking! At a table sat three bright-pink poodles – the exact same colour as Mrs W's outfit. It was as if they'd rolled around in a bath of pink dye ... and then I realised that that's probably exactly what Mrs W had forced them to do! They all looked absolutely miserable.

"Now, everyone, this is Pudseypoos," said Mrs W, waving a hand in my direction.

I frowned. "What's with the *Pudseypoos*?" I barked.

But she just carried on talking. "Pudseypoos, this is Flossy." She pointed to the poodle with a purple bow in its hair.

"Hello," replied Flossy in a husky tone.

"And Fuzzy-Cheeks . . . "

"Alright," answered Fuzzy-Cheeks, his voice deep and echoing.

"And Princess Peach Pringle," Mrs W finished with a giggle.

"Kill me now," croaked the princess, who wore a terrible bright cerise tutu.

Despite their colour and flouncy pink outfits, it was clear that these dogs were all male! What kind of crazy was this woman?!

But Mrs W either hadn't seen how scared I looked or didn't care at all, and she clapped her ring-covered hands together excitedly. "Oh, we're going to have so much fun today."

Huh? What about the food? I looked back at the

poodles. Although they sat at a dining table, there wasn't a morsel of a meal in sight!

"We're going to curl your tail, and then we're going to paint your nails, and then we're going to take you to the vet for a snippy snip snip-snip-snip." She snipped her fingers together menacingly, laughing.

By now, the alarm bells ringing in my head were so loud I could barely think.

"Save yourself, Pudsey!" cried Flossy.

Fuzzy-Cheeks stuck out his pink-ribboned head. "No, save us!"

"Get me out of this tutu!" pleaded Princess Peach Pringle.

What should I do? I looked around the room, suddenly noticing the hundreds of photo frames and ornaments that adorned the walls and shelves. The frames contained pictures of Mrs W squeezing the life out of different dressed-up dogs, and the ornaments seemed to be miniature replicas of them. But what had happened to all of her pets? Why weren't they here now? I didn't want to hang around to find out!

"But first, you stinky little Pudseypoos," Mrs W continued, pressing her fingers together, "I'm going to give you a bubble bath … "

Yeah, I thought. *Not likely.* "See ya!" I barked, weaving past her feet. I got to the front door. "Come on, guys!" I yelled. I had to at least *try* and save them.

My paws fumbled at the door handle, heart beating in panic as I heard Mrs W call out behind me. Finally, the door swung open.

"We've got to get out of here!" I shouted, but the poodles were still nowhere to be seen.

"Where are you going, Pudsey?" Mrs W cried in her jittery voice. "Pudsey!"

She's nuts. She's a fruitcake! I leapt down the front garden steps and rushed out into the road, checking for cars before I sprinted across it. (One run-in a day was enough for me!) "Bye!" I barked as I ran.

Although I didn't dare look back, I heard her whining voice calling after me in the street. "Don't go, Pudsey, don't go. Look, I made you your own sparkly ribbon ... Oh, no, nooooooo!"

Her cries were suddenly joined by the distinctive bark of poodles (I could tell immediately it was the poodles – they are always high-pitched and yappy). The other dogs must have escaped too. *Go, Flossy, Fuzzy-Cheeks and Princess Peach Pringle!*

Mrs W's voice became even more desperate. "Noooooo! Come back! Come back! Oh, my doggy-woggies!"

Bubble bath? Snip-snip? I said to myself as I rounded a corner. Mrs W's frenzied shouts turned into long crying sobs. *I need somewhere to hide!*

I spotted the open doors of a trailer parked outside Molly's house. "Ooh, she'll never find me in here!" I barked as I leapt in over some boxes piled up on the road outside. I told you I was an expert gymnast! I settled down at the back of the trailer. I'd wait here for a few minutes until the coast was clear.

Then I heard voices emerging from the house. "Hurry, hurry – cos I really don't want to get there in the dark." What was going on?

I peeked over some boxes to see Molly and George loading more stuff into the trailer, blocking out most of the light – and my way out!

"Did you double check under the beds?" their mum asked. Then I heard a slam, and the last of the light disappeared from the trailer. I was shut in – and it was really dark in here!

Don't panic, I told myself. *I'll find a way out.* But before I could even start trying to push through the boxes to the door, I heard the rumble of a car engine. *Uh-oh!* OK, so I'd got away from Mrs W at least, but where were we going, and where were my sausages?!

CHAPTER SIX

The journey in the trailer was one of the worst of my life. Every time it rounded a corner, I had to push hard against the boxes to make sure I didn't get squashed. I couldn't even take a nap to make the time pass quicker. Plus, it was pitch black in there. I don't mind admitting, I'm not too keen on the dark – I'm a dog, for Pug's sake, not an owl or a bat! There was something hard, I guessed a hammer or screwdriver, right underneath my paws, which made sitting very uncomfortable indeed. I just couldn't move in the tiny space, no matter how hard I tried.

Worst of all, my stomach was rumbling so badly by now that I was surprised the family couldn't hear it above their car's engine. I tried opening the box to my left, desperately hoping there would be some food inside. I felt for the tape with my paws and gripped the end in my teeth, tearing it off in one jerky movement. I shook my head. *Gah!* I hadn't done this kind of rooting around since I'd once got trapped inside a recycling bin. (Tip: if you're going to fall into a bin while escaping from an angry corner-shop owner, try to choose the one marked 'food waste' and not the one marked 'clothes'.) I felt inside the box, wondering if my luck had finally changed and I'd stumble upon a packet of sausages – though even just a loaf of bread or a box of cereal would have done. Worryingly, I couldn't smell a thing.

I pushed my paws deeper into the box. I could feel paper. Blocks of paper. It was a box of books! I sighed. Don't get me wrong, I'm all for reading, and go to the library as often as I can (the librarian, Mrs Greenwood always gives me a few Hobnobs and a bowl of water), but books were no good to me right then. I couldn't *eat* paper – and I couldn't even read to pass the time, not in the dark!

I slumped back down as the trailer rumbled on. *How long will I be in here?* I wondered. *Will I starve to death?* It seemed a very real possibility – there was no sign of the car stopping.

Then I heard a screech as the car turned and I was flung between the boxes. The trailer began shuddering, up and down, up and down, and I clung on to the book box for fear of hitting the roof with one of the bumps. "Ow! What was that?" I barked.

I felt like a hamster in a rolling ball. When would this stop? My bottom would be battered and bruised if this carried on, not to mention the damage to my beautifully fluffed tail.

Bump, bump, bumpity-bump – it went on. Just

when I thought I couldn't cope any more, there came one final bump, bigger than all the rest, throwing everything around in the trailer. *Bang!* came a noise from outside. Then all was still and silent. What was happening now?

Hissssssssssssssssssssssssssssssssssssssssssssss ...

That sounded just like a snake! Nasty, slithery things – I'd rather starve in the trailer than venture outside if there were snakes waiting for me. Then I heard car doors opening and voices began to argue.

"Perfect, just perfect," said an exasperated voice. It was the mum.

Then came George's voice. "Nice shortcut, dingo!"

"You do know how to change tyres, don't you?" asked Molly.

"Dad did," George replied quietly.

Their mum didn't answer that. There was a silence, then: "Yeah, well, how hard can it be? You

just change the ... erm ... thingy with the thingy."
Even I could tell she didn't really know what she was
talking about.

"Just hurry," said Molly.

George put on a baby voice. "Ah, is little Molly
afraid of the dark, dark woods?"

*What? We're stuck in the woods? Argh – there could
be all sorts in there ... foxes, wolves, bears ... I think I*
will *stay in the trailer!*

"We're in the middle of nowhere," said Molly.
"Literally *anything* could emerge from those trees."

See! Even Molly agreed with me.

Molly and George continued arguing. *Wow*, I
thought, *these kids sound really unhappy.*

"Literally *anything*? What about a giant duck made
of cheese?" George joked.

"Excuse me?"

"You said anything ... What about—"

"Shut up!" Molly snapped.

51

There was a low growl in the distance. A bear? But as it drew closer, I recognised it as the sound of a stuttering engine. Molly and George fell silent. But who was coming? Would they bring help ... or danger?

I slumped in relief when I heard a friendly West-Country voice say: "Yar either lost, or yar the Wilson family."

"Err, yes – I'm Gail, and this is Molly, George and Tommy," their mum replied.

"I'm Jack. I think yar looking for my fahrm. Come on, I'll give yar a tow. We'll change that tyre once we get back on terra firma."

"OK, ummm ... thanks," said Gail.

There were a few more slamming noises and then the trailer began bumping along again. Would this never end? Where exactly was the farm? My stomach gurgled. Wait a minute – I'd forgotten one thing: 'farm' meant pigs, sheep and cows. Maybe my luck on the food front was looking up once more! *So long as I can survive the journey*, I thought. My bones had never rattled about so much.

The trailer finally stopped. I'd made it! I heard the car doors slam. *Come on – let me out too!*

"Here we go," came Jack's voice. "Welcome to Season's End Farm. This is yer cot'age."

"This ... is our new home," said George uncertainly. "This place?"

"It's got character," Molly replied.

"It's got *woodworm*!" George exploded.

"You said you wanted pets," Gail said, trying to laugh.

Pets? What about me? I was starting to panic that they'd never let me out. I'd suffer a long, painful death by starvation amongst cardboard boxes – probably the least glamorous way to die *ever*.

That did it. I summoned up all my remaining energy (not much, since the last time I'd eaten was at least three hours ago!). Then I barked loudly, throwing myself against the boxes. I didn't usually like to be so rude and ungraceful, but I was desperate.

"What was that?" I heard Jack ask.

I crouched down, preparing to lunge at the boxes again – just as the doors opened and light flooded in. At last! I leapt out of the doors, sending boxes flying. I didn't care – I was free! *FREEEEEEEEEE!*

"Pudsey!" shouted George, beaming.

Blimey, there was hardly any air in there! I sucked in a deep breath as I rushed up to George to give him a hug. He stroked me as I stood on my hind legs and patted him with my paws. I'd never been so glad to see anyone in my life!

"You've got a stowaway," said Jack with a grin.

Gail looked less pleased. "How did he get in there?" she asked.

"Don't look at me," said Molly, bending down to pat me as I weaved around the kids, grateful to be able to move after hours of being cooped up like a chicken.

"This structurally unsound hovel is our new home, apparently," George explained to me.

I looked at the house. It did seem as if it needed a bit of TLC, with broken windows and bits of guttering falling from the roof.

"You're going to live with us now," George added.

What? Hang on, not so fast! I hadn't agreed to this. I mean, I liked these kids, but *living with them*? I was an independent dog – not a pet!

It seemed as if Gail agreed with me. "Wait a minute—" she began, but the sound of a beeping horn cut her off. "Oh, great, it's the new landlord," she sighed.

"Who?" I barked, as a green Range Rover pulled into the drive. Wow – it was busier than Piccadilly Circus here!

Gail gave me a stroke and nudged me towards George. "Quick, take the dog inside!" she hissed.

OK ... But it better not be like that pink woman's house!

"I thought Jack was our landlord," said Molly.

"Unfortunately not," replied her mum, through gritted teeth. "It's Mr Thorne – and he said no dogs!"

CHAPTER SEVEN

"Come on, Pudsey." George pushed open the door and I followed him inside.

Ooh, chickens! A couple skittered along the hallway as we entered. I ran after them. *Hhhhmmm ... If there are chickens to chase then maybe I could live here ...*

"Oi, come back, let's play – don't be so chicken!" I called after them as they squawked and waddled away from me.

George reached out to a switch on the wall. "Let there be light!" I looked up at the cobweb-covered light bulb. It buzzed, flashed on for a second, then popped and fizzed out with a puff of smoke. "Umm, yeah . . . " George said. "Maybe not."

I peered down at the feather- and dirt-covered floor. From the looks of the house, maybe it would be better kept in the dark. *This is worse than the dog pound,* I thought with a shudder as I tiptoed over the chicken poo.

In the living room, George began taking sheets off sofas, sending dust flying everywhere. I shoved a paw over my nose (I hate sneezing – so undoglike) and listened to the raised voices that floated through a broken window pane from outside.

"What are you doing here?" came a posh male voice – definitely not Jack. Was this Mr Thorne, their landlord?

"Oh, he's fixing our burst tyre," Gail replied. They must have be talking about Jack.

"Watch out for this one, Gail," Jack said. He didn't

sound very happy. "'E's more slippery than a buttered frog on a banana peel."

Huh? What is Jack talking about? As far as I knew, frogs didn't even like bananas. (I wasn't that keen myself, although I could have eaten one then – heck, I could have eaten a frog at that moment, I was so ravenous!)

"Season's End is part of the family estate," replied Mr Thorne in his plummy voice. "Jack resents the fact I own the land his *little farm* is built on."

"And 'e resents the fact that as his only sit'ing tenant, I won't leave 'n' let 'im 'ave it."

Yikes! These two sounded as if they hated each other. And I had thought the countryside was full of happy people making hay and dancing around maypoles! Maybe not . . .

"You are not 'aving my fahrm!" Jack snarled.

"Really? I wouldn't get too comfortable," Thorne retorted. "You know what they say, Jack, it's a long lane that spoils the broth . . . "

What on earth does that mean? I'd had enough of listening to this human nonsense, and so had George by the bored look on his face. He raced out of the living room and I gave chase as he ran up the stairs and into one of the bedrooms.

"Bagsy my room!" he called out, leaping on to the double bed inside.

Crash! Instead of bouncing up from a springy mattress, George fell right through the bedframe. Bits of broken bed splintered around him and I winced. That had to hurt!

George rolled over and winked at me. "Molly!" he called. "Your bed collapsed!"

Something tickled my nose just then – and it wasn't the dust. I sniffed. "Can you smell that?" I barked. "It smells like – oh, no – it smells like CAT!"

Where was it? Did it live here? I had to find out.

I crept out to the landing just as I heard Thorne say: "Shall we go inside?"

"No, wait, wait – you can't go in the house," Gail replied in a high-pitched, squeaky voice.

But Thorne was already in the hallway, his chest puffed out in his terrible brown tweed suit. It was one of the worst fashion choices I'd ever seen. In fact, it could only have been more disgusting if it was pink!

"Ahhhh, how the splendour falls from castle walls – Tennyson is always with me," Thorne gushed, glancing around with pride.

Oh, *please*. OK, so I know my literature just as much as the next dog, but I wouldn't quote it just to show off. This guy sounded like a million-dollar idiot.

I sniffed. The cat scent was getting stronger. I tiptoed on to the stairs and watched through a broken bannister post as Gail and Molly followed Thorne into the kitchen.

"Ah, I'd forgotten how palatial this place is," Thorne tittered. Was he talking about the same house, I wondered? He took out a clipboard and licked the point of a pencil, then began scribbling. "One designer Dame Thora Hird standard lamp." Thorne added the lamp to his list. "One *blah, blah, blah* . . . and one *blah, blah, blah* . . . " Was he crazy? He was listing every single thing in the house? What did he think we were going to do with his ancient belongings, anyway? But I had more important matters to hand, like that cat!

I tried to tune out his voice as I crept down the stairs, determined to get my paws on that cat. I held my nose in the air and sniffed. It was a short-haired breed, I could tell. Maybe even Siamese? Oh, I did hope so – those were the most fun to chase; they'd happily run around for hours without ever pausing for breath.

". . . and curtains!" Thorne finished. "Now, sign here!"

I'd reached the bottom of the stairs by now. I peered around the stair post and saw Thorne in the kitchen, thrusting his clipboard at Gail. She scribbled on it, then turned towards the sink.

"Gail, I understand you're going to be teaching at the local school." Thorne's voice had changed from commanding to sickly sweet. He was clearly after something. But what?

"Yes, that's right, I start on the first day of term," Gail said.

"What are you doing until then? Only I need some assistance on some clerical matters."

I noticed Gail's face screw up for a split second, before she brought it back under control and smiled. "Oh, I'd *love* to but—"

"I'll give you a discount on your first month's rent," Thorne offered.

Gail hesitated. "Well, if you put it like that ... "

Molly had gone to pour herself a glass of water, but the tap squeaked as she tried to turn it. Water dribbled out – yellow water. She held up the glass. Were they ... tadpoles swimming inside? Yuk – even I wouldn't drink that!

"Ah, spring water, full of extra vitamins and minerals and *things*," Thorne said hastily.

"It's the *things* I'm worried about," said Molly, turning her nose up in disgust.

I'd had enough chatter – where was this cat? It was close, I could tell by my twitching nose. I sniffed ... and sniffed ... *Yes, it's really near now!* I couldn't hold back any more – I ran through the kitchen doorway, forgetting that I was meant to stay hidden. What can I say? This kitty scent had driven me demented! "Where's that cat?" I barked. "I can smell it – *woof*! I know it's here! Where is it?"

Thorne gasped, his mouth gaped open. *Uh-oh*. He crouched down and stared at me, his eyes like saucers. Oops – I knew he wasn't meant to see me, but I was still thinking of the cat! I barked again. "Where is it?"

Meowwwww! Ah! There it was, just behind Thorne on the table. And I was right – it was Siamese!

"Come here, you!" I yelled.

"Pudsey, nooo!" cried Gail, as I darted through the kitchen and leapt towards the cat. The annoying feline spotted me coming and leapt through an open window, its fur standing on end. (There's one thing I don't like about cats. They don't like being caught.) Unfortunately for me, I was so caught up in the chase that I leapt on to the kitchen table, catching Thorne with my paw and pushing him to the floor.

"Sorry!" I said. (Well, it's important to remember your manners, whatever the situation.)

Thorne slumped, groaning. This was a disaster! I'd really gone and done it. But then I spotted Molly and Gail. They were trying to hide their laughter behind their hands. Maybe I could turn this into a joke and I wouldn't be in trouble, after all.

"I'd watch him," I said, glancing at Thorne. "I don't think he likes dogs." Talk about understatement of the year!

CHAPTER EIGHT

A few moments later, Thorne picked himself up off the floor and stumbled out of the house. Gail scooped me up and followed him out, carrying me in her arms. I tell you, there aren't many people willing to pick me up!

"Oh, I hate dogs," he moaned as he trudged towards his Range Rover. "Big dogs, small dogs, shih-tzus, Dalmatians, Alsatians, boxers, beagles, Labradors, dachshunds, Maltese, Bernese . . ."

Gail opened her mouth to speak, but Thorne just kept on complaining. "Mastiffs, pugs, chow chows, cocker spaniels, collies, terriers, giant schnauzers, miniature schnauzers. Do you understand?"

"Yes—" Gail managed to say but she was immediately cut off again by Thorne.

"I even hate things that *remind* me of dogs," he said as he leant on the bonnet of his car, his face as red as a robin's breast. "Dogfish. The Dog Star. Religious dogma. The *bark of trees . . .* "

I stared at the deranged man. *What IS he going on about?*

"I despise dogs, and everything to do with dogs!" Thorne held out a trembling finger and pointed at me. "Including that filthy specimen!" he spat.

"I'm sorry. I'll sort it – I promise," said Gail quietly, hugging me even tighter.

"And on top of everything else," he blubbed, "I've lost my cat!"

So the Siamese I'd been chasing was *his* cat. *Ooops.*

Thorne groaned a final time, got into his car and slammed the door.

"Honestly, what a fuss," I said to myself as the engine revved and Thorne drove away.

As the car disappeared down the track, Jack appeared beside me and Gail. It was almost as though he'd been hiding, waiting for Thorne to leave. "It's as good as new," he said.

What? Oh, yes, the car tyre – what with all the cat fuss, I'd forgotten.

Gail turned to him, smiling with relief. "Thanks, Jack."

Yeah, thanks, Jack. He seemed like a much nicer chap compared to Mr 'I hate dogs' Thorne.

"Don't worry about 'im." He held up an oily rag in Thorne's direction as his Range Rover sped along the country lanes. "He's all bark . . . and no bite."

Gail laughed. "Ironic."

I gave a chuckle too – it was a pretty good joke.

"OK, well, I'll be at the main house if you need anything." Jack waved and walked off, and Gail turned back to watch Thorne's car disappear into the hills in the distance.

She gave me a pat. "Well then, let's break the news."

"Fine, but you're doing all the talking," I barked quietly.

Inside the cottage, Gail set me down in the living room.

"Pudsey, come on, Pudsey," called George cheerily. I wagged my tail and jumped up on to the faded sofa between him and Tommy. Well, who doesn't like to be wanted?

Gail stood in front of us, her hands clasped behind her back. "He wants us to get rid of Pudsey," she announced. No warning, just came straight out with it! There was a shocked silence, then:

"What? Mum, we can't – please . . . " pleaded Molly as she perched on an arm of the sofa.

"He doesn't have anywhere else to go," said George.

I tilted my head at Gail and gave her my big doggy eyes as George pulled me on to his lap. Then I stopped myself. *Wait – nowhere to go? I'm going to see the world, me! The Empire Sausage Building. The Great Sausage of China. Sausage Henge . . .*

As I daydreamed, the kids were giving their mum the saddest faces I'd ever seen on a group of human beings. Gail looked from one to the other, then closed her eyes and gave a deep sigh. "OK, OK," she said at last. "He can stay in the old barn in the back of the yard."

"Yesssss – thanks, Mum!" Molly patted my head and beamed.

"For *now*," Gail added, in a warning tone. She bent down and fixed her eyes on mine. "But stay out of trouble."

What, me? I always do!

George rubbed my belly. "Welcome to the family, matey," he whispered in my ear.

I looked up at Gail. "Now, tell me about this barn," I barked. "Is it comfy? Is it warm? Are there hot and cold running sausages? I'm starving!"

Later that evening, things seemed less happy in the new Wilson household. *Hhhhmmm* ... Perhaps a new dog wasn't quite enough to sort out their troubles. Not even a dog as gorgeous as me!

"Muummm, what kind of hellhole have you brought us to?" moaned George as he wandered into Gail's bedroom. She was looking through old photo frames in a box while I was sat on a (surprisingly comfy) armchair in the corner of the room. Gail had already repeatedly told me I should be in the barn but she clearly didn't understand the number one rule with dogs – they will always find the most com-fortable spot in the house. Plus, I quite liked hanging out with her and the kids. "I can't even get a signal in here," George added, holding up his games console.

"You shouldn't even be on that thing," Gail said as she walked over to her four-poster bed and turned back the covers. I noticed her shudder slightly.

"I'll *die* if I can't play online with my friends," he complained.

"What happened to good ol'-fashioned games like Scrabble?" Gail plonked down in bed and patted the mattress next to her. She'd clearly decided to make the best of the sagging old bed. "Come on, in you get."

"OK." George grinned and leapt beneath the duvet, tucking himself in. Molly strolled into the room, wearing a huge woolly cardigan. She had her arms folded and she didn't look happy.

Gail spotted the look on her face. "Oh, now what?"

"It's my bed. It smells like phlegm." *Urgh – yuk!* I thought. I wouldn't want to sleep in that either.

Gail pulled back the duvet on the other side of her bed and jerked her chin towards the mattress. Molly didn't need inviting twice and her face broke out in a grin as she leapt into the bed beside her brother. Gail climbed in too, pulling everyone to her in a big hug. She looked from Molly to George and gave a deep sigh. "I know it's a big change. But we got used to Dad dying, didn't we?"

So that's *why they're all so sad.* This was the first time I'd heard what had happened to their father.

Molly stole a glance at her mum. "Tommy didn't get used to it." Where was Tommy anyway? The last time I'd seen him, he'd been alone in his bedroom. My heart gave a little twist.

Gail stroked Molly's hair. "He will, he will. Just give him a chance. Everything's going to be fine."

Just as she said that, bits of ceiling began to crumble on to the duvet and George giggled.

Gail raised her eyebrows and smiled. "Well, eventually." Her glance settled on me. "Now go on, Pudsey. Out to the barn with you."

As much as I wanted to join them in the bed, I knew when I shouldn't push things. We'd only just started getting to know each other, after all. I jumped down from the chair, gave a goodbye bark, and padded out of the bedroom. I peeked into Tommy's room as I crossed the landing. He was still there, lying on his bed, wide awake, his brown eyes big and sad. Poor, silent Tommy.

Out in the barn, I tried to get comfortable. "Look at this – straw! Really? Who knows *what* slept on here!" It was prickly and tickly too – how would I ever get any Zs on this?

As I tried for the seventy-third time to lie down in

a comfy spot, I heard something talking. "Huh? Who's that?" I barked to myself.

"Eat more slowly, Edward. You'll get indigestion," came a female voice.

"If I eat any slower, dearest, I won't be eating at all!" I guessed this was Edward.

"At least I won't have to listen to you crunching!"

"I can't help crunching."

"How anyone can manage to crunch hay is beyond me. It's bad enough the way you grind your teeth in your sleep!"

"At least I don't snore."

"What's that?!" the female said grumpily.

Too curious to sleep at all now, I scampered to the other end of the barn. Maybe these animals had some food to share! Two horses stood there, munching at a bale of hay. Urgh! No way was I eating that prickly stuff.

"I say," said the female, looking up and noticing me. "Hello. Who are you?"

I didn't waste a moment introducing myself. "I'm Pudsey! Some call me Pudsey the mega-dog!" I said proudly.

"Well, I'm Nelly, and this is Edward."

"The mega-*horse*," Edward cut in.

Nelly gave him a withering look. "Oh, be quiet, Edward."

"Yes, dear."

A clucking noise started up. "Cluck-cluuuck-cluck-cluck!" I jumped up on to a straw bale, looked over to the opposite side of the barn and saw a ... *pig*?!

"Cluck, cluck, everyone," said a deep, distinctly non-chicken-like voice.

I frowned. "Is that pig making *chicken* noises?"

"Ken has an identity crisis," Edward explained.

"We call him the Full English Breakfast," added Nelly, rolling her eyes.

"Funny! Not. When are you gonna respect my lifestyle choices?" moaned Ken.

Edward lifted his head up. "Ken, you are *not* a chicken!" The horse sounded extremely fed up, as if this wasn't the first time he'd tried to tell Ken this.

"If I'm not a chicken, how come I'm always laying eggs?"

Nelly sighed and gave me a long-suffering look. "Those aren't eggs."

I looked over to beneath Ken's behind. There was a small, steaming pile of brown ... I gave a shudder.

What? Does she mean that poop? He thinks he's laying eggs? Yuk! "I was going to ask for some food, but I've finally lost my appetite," I told them. "See ya!" I jumped down from the straw bale and ran back to my 'bed' at the other end of the barn. Maybe I'd be able to sleep now that my belly had stopped grumbling.

"Huh! What's his problem?" I heard Ken ask in the distance. He really had no idea!

As my eyelids began to droop at last, I spotted something out of the corner of my eye. Tommy, in his pyjamas, was walking towards me with a bowl. He set it down just in front of my nose, and gave me a small, sad smile. I lifted my head. "Oooh, custard creams – thanks, Tommy!" I couldn't believe it. Maybe Tommy didn't want to be on his own all the time. He'd made the effort to come and bring me some supper, after all. I sniffed at the biscuits. Perhaps a little snack before bedtime ...

Tommy turned to go, looking over his shoulder at me as he left the barn. I tilted my head to the side, trying to read his mind, wishing there was something I could do to cheer him up. I didn't think a spot of dog dancing would work, somehow. But I could see he liked me. My mind was made up. *I'll help him! I'll do whatever it takes!* I just needed to figure out how.

CHAPTER NINE

This is the life!

The sun shone over glistening, emerald fields. I scampered through the grass, chasing butterflies. It was a beautiful morning, the sky a perfect blue. I took a huge lungful of the fresh country air, enjoying the thrill of racing across open countryside, bigger and better than any park I'd ever played in. Then I spotted something in the distance – a giant, blurred shape.

"Pudsey," someone faintly called my name. "Pudsey . . ."

The shape came into a focus – it was a giant sausage, running across the field! The biggest sausage I'd ever seen. I imagined sinking my teeth into its juicy meat.

"Pudsey," it called again, "you can't catch me ... "

We'll see about that! I changed direction and began racing towards the sausage as it sprinted across the field. "Pudsey ... catch me!"

I could feel my mouth drooling, tongue lolling out of my jaws as I ran. I was almost there, the giant sausage within lunging distance, when: "Come on, Pudsey! COME ON, PUDSEY – wake up!" The voice had changed to – to ... George!

"What? Frankfurters!" I yelled, waking up suddenly. I rolled over and fell off the hay bale. "Ouch!" I cried from the floor. I stood up, realising that the giant sausage was only a dream. "I'm all right!"

"We're going into the village to get *breakfast*," said

Molly with a smile, her arm around Tommy's shoulders.

"Well, why didn't you say?" I barked. "That's one of my favourite meals!"

They laughed. Did they understand Dog?

"Well, my favourite after brunch . . . and lunch . . ." I added, "and high tea . . . and supper . . ." I scrambled over the hay bale and raced out of the barn. "And pre-dinner . . . and second breakfast . . ."

"Have fun in the village, everyone," Edward called after us, even though I was the only one who could understand him.

"*Lovely* family," said Nelly.

"Not as lovely as me!" Ken interrupted. "If there was a world's loveliest chicken competition, I'd win it, wings down!"

"The only thing you're ever going to win is the world's *looniest pig*!" said Edward.

"Huh, charming," grumbled Ken.

I left the other animals to bicker amongst themselves. Nelly was right – these kids were a lovely family, and hopefully they'd buy me breakfast!

Molly, George, Tommy and I wandered through the fields towards the village. *What will breakfast be? I* wondered. *A bacon sandwich? A sausage roll? Maybe even a full English fry-up?!* I drooled at the thought.

"The village is so cute," said Molly as we reached the green. It was surrounded by cottages, a pub and some shops. Maybe the kids could enjoy living here, after all.

George was less impressed. "It's so *boring.*"

But I was distracted by a wonderful smell my nose had sniffed out. It didn't take long to work out where it was coming from. I stared at the shop in front of me. In the window was the biggest pie I'd ever seen – bigger than me, even – wrapped in a giant red ribbon. "It's so *tasty . . .*" I said, reading the sign: 'World's Biggest Steak Pie'. Amazing – it was like all my dreams had come true at once. This was even better than a giant sausage!

"Pudsey, don't you dare," said Molly behind me. *How did she guess?*

I turned to face her. "But, Molly, look at it! It's perfection, in *pie* form!" I looked back at the pie, taking in the gorgeous golden pastry. "I want it. I need to live the *pie* life. George, tell her!"

As I stared longingly at the pie in the window, ready and waiting for me to take an enormous, delicious bite, a lady emerged from the shop and began talking to Molly, George and Tommy. "A whopper, isn't it?" She pointed to a man in a white chef's hat and jacket working inside. "Peter makes his giant pie every year for the village fete!"

Peter came to the door. "I'm finally taking the record from those smug Norwegians, Mary." He marched out of the shop, a determined look on his face. "I'm coming for you, Svennigsen!" I could only assume that the Norwegians made very good pies. Maybe a visit to Norway was in my future.

Molly laughed, and Peter turned to her, George and Tommy.

"New to the area?" he asked, smiling.

Molly nodded. "I'm Molly –and this is Tommy, George and Pudsey. We just moved into Tumbledown Cottage."

"Oh, Will here helps out on Jack's farm sometimes." Mary gestured to a teenager walking towards us, swinging a large basket in his hand.

"What's that?" said Will in a thick West-Country accent.

Mary nodded at the kids. "They've just moved to Season's End."

As Molly looked at Will, her cheeks flushed scarlet. "Wow, that is a massive cucumber," she said, nodding to the vegetables in his basket.

He grinned. "It's a marrow."

"Obviously," said Molly, her face growing even redder.

Uh-oh – Molly liked this boy, I could tell!

"Here we go again . . . " said George.

As Mary started talking about the upcoming village fete I turned my attention back to the pie. Two voices began to rage war in my head.

"Don't do it, Pudsey, you're not even hungry!" said Saint Pudsey.

Evil Pudsey had other ideas. "Go for it, Pudsey. Eat that delicious pie. You know you want to."

"Ignore him, Pudsey!" Saint Pudsey yelled. "He's just a troublemaker."

"Oh, shut up, you! You're so boring! You never want to have any fun!"

"Fun! Getting into trouble is fun, is it?"

Evil Pudsey laughed. "It is when food's involved. Go on, Pudsey."

"Pudsey, no!"

My head was spinning! "Belt up, you two," I told the voices. I had to make a decision one way or another. Saint Pudsey or Evil Pudsey? That pie did look delicious, and as my mouth watered I knew the decision had been made. *Here goes nothing. PIE-RONIMO!* I darted into the shop, my heart beating with delicious pie anticipation. I glanced around – no one inside was watching – so I jumped up to the window ledge where the pie sat. I gazed lovingly at it for a moment, then took a bite of the scrumptious pie crust.

Mmmmmmmmmm ... yummmmmmmmmm ... mmmmm ... mmmmmm ... It was the most incredible melt-in-your-mouth pastry, leading to juicy chunks of beef in thick, perfectly seasoned gravy. I dug my nose inside – I couldn't get enough. After the lean pickings I'd had up to this moment, it truly felt as if I'd died and gone to heaven – and I don't say that lightly. As I reached further and further inside for a fresh mouthful, I felt my whole body tip over and land in the warm goo of the gravy. I could have stayed in that pie all day.

It wasn't long before I was licking the last remaining drop of gravy from the pie insides. *Well, that filled a hole. What's for pudding?* I gave a sigh of satisfaction and my attention started to re-focus on the world outside of the pie. Someone was calling me. I felt a prickle of anxiety. Should I really have listened to Evil Pudsey?

"Right, Pudsey?" came George's voice through my gravy-filled ears. "*Pudsey?*"

I took a deep breath and stuck up my head above the pie crust. "Yes?" I tried to look innocent, but the gravy in my whiskers probably wasn't helping.

George, Molly, Tommy, Peter and Mary all stared at me through the window.

"Oh my goodness, Peter, what's happened to your pie?!" squealed Mary.

Uh-oh. How did I explain this one?

CHAPTER TEN

I quickly realised there wasn't an explanation in the world that would work. It was time to make my escape.

"Coming through!" I barked, jumping down from the window ledge and shaking off droplets of pie gravy.

"Stop that dog!" yelled Peter, but it was too late. I rushed out of the pie shop and towards the village green, straight between Peter's legs. "Watch out!" I cried, trying to warn him – but it was too late. Peter tripped over me and fell head first into the water feature outside the shop.

I kept on going – I knew when I was in trouble! I darted in front of a large vehicle, then winced as I heard the screech of tyres and a horn blast out. I looked back for a split second – it was Thorne in his Range Rover, his face its familiar beetroot colour, his fist raised in fury. *Whoops.* He'd had to hit the brakes hard. Learn from my mistakes, don't ever run out into the road.

I couldn't stop now. I headed towards the green, jumping through a stepladder set up against a telephone box. "Whoaaaaaaaaa!" shouted the workman on the ladder as it toppled and crashed down on to Thorne's car bonnet. A paint pot flew into the air, then landed on the car, covering it in an explosion of red paint.

From the safety of the village green, I turned to look at the destruction I'd left behind me. "Oops," I said quietly. Mary and Will were dragging Peter out of the water feature. Thorne had turned on his windscreen wipers, but that only made matters worse. Red paint was smeared all over the glass and his face turned angrier than a wasp stuck in a drink can.

"It's not my week..." I said to myself, covering my eyes with a paw.

"Stay out of trouble," Gail said sternly, as George, Molly, Tommy and I sat on the sofa in front of her. "That's all I asked."

"Sorry, Mum," said Molly.

George looked up. "Sorry, Mum."

"Sorry, Mum," I barked quietly. There was nothing worse than seeing the look of disappointment on her face.

Gail paced the room. "I think you need to learn some responsibility. So I've organised for you to do some work around the farm."

Molly smiled. "Will!"

Will?

"Will what?" Gail asked.

Ah, this should be good, I thought. Her mum had no idea about Molly's new crush, but I'd guessed after her face had turned so red. What would Molly tell her mum?

"Err ... w-will," Molly stuttered, "will ... we ... be ... doing some work on the farm? Yes, we *will!*" She giggled nervously and turned to the rest of us slumped on the sofa.

"Oh, you will, you will," her mum replied, her head going up and down like a nodding toy dog. "Before that ... " Gail picked up two buckets filled with cleaning stuff and plonked them on the coffee table between us, " ... you guys can get started cleaning this place up."

We all groaned in unison. *Cleaning? Urgh!*

Gail grabbed her shopping bags and car keys from

the worktop. "I'll be back in a couple of hours!" she called breezily as she strode out of the front door. It was almost as though she didn't care that we were going to have to clean the house from top to bottom!

Come on, kids, I thought. *We don't really have to clean, do we?*

But Molly was already on her feet. OK, this was really going to happen. I guess I did feel guilty about the scene I'd caused in the village. Yeah, maybe it was time to pay for what Evil Pudsey had made me do. I jumped down from the sofa and stood next to Molly. But there was no way I was going anywhere near the toilet!

"I'll start with the kitchen," she sighed. "That's the most disgusting room of all."

"Ooh, good idea," I barked. "You never know, we might find some titbits in there – half a French baguette at the back of a cupboard, a Cumberland sausage left in the oven ... "

Molly went through to the kitchen, as the others went upstairs. She was soon filling a bin liner with broken plates and bowls, while I did some sweeping (finding a few cracker crumbs behind the refrigerator and a half-eaten carrot under the radiator). While Molly mopped the floor, I licked the dirty plates next to the sink. We were a great team!

I left Molly to finish the kitchen while I ran up the stairs to see what George and Tommy were doing. They were in one of the bedrooms, throwing out stacks of old newspapers and clothes. I spotted a ball on the floor. *Look what I've found!* I kicked it to George, but he was too busy to play, heaving a full bin bag up on to his shoulder. I stuck my head under the bed instead. *Oooh, an orange!* I munched on it hungrily. *That's another thing tidied up!*

I ran to the door of the next room – Molly's bedroom. She was in there now, stripping the bed. I wandered further inside and sniffed, picking up a scent. There was something in here. Not a chicken, but some other kind of bird ... I followed my nose to the wardrobe, and poked it open. *Aha – a goose!*

"Argh!" screamed Molly, as the goose flapped out of the wardrobe doors. I started chasing it around the bedroom. "What's that doing in here?"

Before I could get close to the squawking bird, Molly lunged and grabbed it, tucking it beneath her arm. Not bad for a city girl! She carried it downstairs and outside. *Oh – I was only playing!* I wish she'd let me chase that goose a bit more.

I padded into the living room, where Tommy and George were battling with the Hoover. It was currently puffing *out* dust rather than sucking it *in*. "Come on, boys!" I barked, jumping on to it and releasing the cover. The bag sprung out and broke open, covering the floor with dirt and hair balls. "See, it's full!"

"Oh, great, thanks, Pudsey," George said.

"You're welcome!" I barked.

I raced back upstairs, where Molly had gone into Gail's room. She had her head deep inside her mum's wardrobe. "Come on, Whiskers," she said quietly.

Whiskers? I hoped she wasn't talking to me. I *had* thought these kids were pretty cool with names – they only ever called me Pudsey (no sign of 'Pudseypoos', thank dogness!), and I was hoping to train them to call me 'Pudsey the mega-dog' very soon.

Molly jumped back as a hare darted out of the wardrobe. "Got ya!" she yelled.

I didn't even try to chase the hare as it sped away, out of the bedroom. Well, you know what they say about hares: they're faster than a cheetah with its tail on fire ... and those goofy teeth sure can bite! I left Molly to catch that one.

It took a long time to clean the house. I felt utterly exhausted by the time we'd finished every room. But even if I did say so myself, now their new home looked spotless! Gail would be due back any moment, and we wanted to surprise her so we hid in the kitchen, waiting for her to return. It wasn't long before we heard a key in the lock. We could just see the hallway from our hiding place.

She pushed open the door, loaded down with shopping bags. "Ohhhh, wow ... WOW!" she gasped as she saw everything looking so neat and tidy. "Look at this." She dropped her bags to the floor.

Wow is right! I thought. *And it's all our own work!*

Gail spotted us and ran over to hug Molly, George and Tommy. I jumped on the sofa to reach up and join in. I wasn't missing this! But they all toppled backwards – right on me!

Oi, watch it! I leapt out from under their bottoms. *I'm not a cushion!*

"This looks amazing," said Gail, staring around at the kitchen, her eyes sparkling as she took it all in.

Molly patted her knees at me, and I leapt up on her lap. *That's better!*

"So you like it?" Molly asked her mum as she gave me a stroke.

"I love it!"

"Good!" Molly giggled. George and Tommy both grinned with pleasure.

"I can't believe it," Gail continued, her voice squeaky. "It must have taken you ages! Where did you find the Hoover?"

"George found it!" I barked. "It was a good job – I couldn't have got the house clean without it!"

We sat on the sofa for ages – chatting, laughing and telling Gail all about the house clean-up. I looked around at their smiling faces, and my chest swelled with pride. Finally, the family seemed happier. *Pudsey the mega-dog to the rescue!*

CHAPTER ELEVEN

The next morning, it wasn't a cockerel that woke me up, but Ken.

"Cluck, cluck. Cluck, cluck, cluck," he ... erm ... *clucked* outside the barn at the crack of dawn. I'd tried stuffing straw into my ears, but instead of muffling the sound, it just made them tickle. In the end I gave in, got up from my bed and ran into the yard to see what all the fuss was about.

"Cluck, cluck, cluckity-cluck." Ken was snuffling around the horses' stable. "Cluck, cluck, cluck."

"Ken, please, would you mind?" called Nelly.

"Sorry, Nell. Just doing what comes natural."

Edward stuck his head out of the stable door. "My dear friend, there's nothing remotely natural about you," he said between mouthfuls of hay.

"Here, what d'ya reckon the chances are of Jack building me me own chicken coop?" Ken asked.

"I think it's more likely he'll build you a padded cell."

I'd had enough of this nonsense. I wandered into the house. It must be breakfast time by now.

I was in luck! Gail was clearing away the breakfast bowls while George and Tommy sat on the sofa in the kitchen. I spotted half a slice of toast on the table, stood up on my hind legs and snaffled it before anyone could notice. Big mistake. *Urgh, Marmite, yuk!* But I couldn't spit it out now – that would be terrible manners. I took a big swallow, forcing the toast down.

"Farm work? Really?" George was complaining as

he pulled on some wellington boots. "*And* after we've cleared up the whole house. This is borderline abuse!"

Gail sighed. "Stop complaining. It'll keep you out of mischief while I go to work at Mr Thorne's."

I heard footsteps and turned to see Molly walking into the room. At least I thought it was Molly – although with the strange frilly clothes, a blue feather hat and turquoise-painted eyelids it was hard to tell.

Gail stopped cleaning the breakfast things for a moment and looked at Molly. "Oh, darling, you look *lovely*," she said.

Molly beamed and her cheeks flushed. "Thanks, Mum."

"Shut the front door," said George as Tommy smiled and shook his head. "She's finally gone vintage nuts!"

"I think she looks like a blueberry!" I barked.

Molly ignored George's comments and turned to her mum. "Well, I'm ready."

"Ready for what? Cirque du Soleil?" her brother joked.

Ha ha – that was pretty funny. But I tried to keep a straight face as Molly scowled at her brother.

"The loony-bin rave party?" George continued.

"Or maybe she wants to be a Smurf?" I suggested.

Molly rolled her eyes and walked out, her mum watching her closely.

"Has she met a boy already?" Gail asked.

We all nodded.

Gail took a deep breath. "Oh god. I'd better get some extra tissues in."

I followed Molly outside. Will was pushing an empty wheelbarrow across the yard.

"Will, wait up!" Molly called. "We're helping you at the farm today!" She skipped along behind him.

"Yeah, Jack said." Will glanced at Molly then turned his eyes back to the wheelbarrow.

Molly flapped her hands at her dress. Something told me she wanted Will to notice the effort she'd made. "Should be fun," she said, hopefully.

"Yeah, should be great," Will replied.

Was I imagining things, or was Will trying not to smirk? He certainly seemed intent on avoiding Molly's gaze.

Molly giggled – you know, one of those fake laughs that are meant to be attractive but end up sounding weird? Unfortunately, even dogs do them. "I-I'm really looking forward to it." *Giggle, giggle.*

"Riiight. So *that's* why you're dressed like a . . . " Will mumbled the last words to himself, so I didn't catch them, but I'm pretty sure he wasn't giving Molly a compliment. I felt sorry for Molly, but I can't say I was surprised – she looked like she'd dressed to be extra in a Victorian film, not a farm hand for the day!

Will carried on towards the cow shed, Molly trailing in his wake. I trotted behind them and George and Tommy joined us. We were soon all in the cow shed and Will began showing George how to milk a cow.

"So take a firm 'old of the teat, and then squeeze as ya move yer 'and down," he explained, as he sat on a low, wooden stool beside the swell of a cow's stomach.

I looked on, confused. "There are easier ways to get milk, you know," I barked. "Ever heard of a supermarket?"

Will stood up, and George took his place on the little stool, his shoulders heaving – he seemed to be half-gagging, half-laughing.

"Don't worry – her udders can take it." Will leant over and pulled on the udders. Milk shot out into the bucket below. It was . . . disgusting! "Ya see?"

"Aha," George managed.

Will stepped away. "Now you 'ave a go." I didn't envy George, I've got to say.

He reached out towards the cow and grabbed an udder, screwing up his face like an elephant's behind. "Urgh – it feels like it's alive."

Jack laughed. "That's cos it is! That's it . . . *squeeze* the teat."

George suddenly burst out laughing, letting go of the udder and flinging himself backwards on his stool. He fell to the floor. "I'm sorry, I can't," he giggled from the straw-covered ground. "It's just that every time you say 'teat' . . . I mean . . . hee hee hee!" He leant back on to a hay bale as Molly rolled her eyes.

I looked at the cow, who was unusually quiet (she hadn't so much as mooed once!). What if the kids got bored, milking her? Who would they try to milk next? *I'm getting out of here before it's me!*

I ran out and over to the horse stables. "Morning, Eddie!" I called.

Edward poked his head out of the stable door. "Morning, ol' boy! Still here then?" He sounded surprised.

"I can't leave now, Eddie," I told him. "They'd be lost without me. You know what humans are like. They get so attached!"

Eddie nodded. "I know. It's such a curse being so cute!"

"Lads, lads." Ken appeared around the corner of the stables. "I've been giving it some thought ..."

"Here we go," said Eddie, his voice thick with boredom.

"... and I think I've got it at last. I know how to lay an egg. Right, brace yourselves."

"No, don't!" I barked.

But Ken squatted down anyway.

"No, Ken!"

Eddie and I turned away, but we could still hear the splatter of pig poo on the ground.

"Uurrrggh, Ken!" I yelled as Eddie shook his head and disappeared inside his stables.

"I really thought I'd nailed it this time," Ken said.

See – I told you. You'll never meet a loopier pig than Ken, I guarantee.

To get away from the stench of pig poo, I raced back into the barn to see how the kids were getting on. But I stayed at the door this time – figuring they couldn't try to milk me from there.

George was still rolling around on the floor laughing. Molly had taken his place on the milking stool.

"What is it you said? Squeeze down?" Molly asked Will as she reached out to the udders.

"Yeah – so take them at the top, hold yer fingers like that, keep the pressure on and squeeze yer bottom fingers, and down and ..."

"Urgh!" Molly yelled. Instead of squirting into the bucket, the milk had somehow hit her face instead. She jumped from the stool and danced around, wiping at her cheeks with a frill of her dress. "That is every kind of wrong! Gross!"

The cow turned her head and mooed loudly. "You're not exactly Megan Fox, *sweetheart,*" she said haughtily. Thank goodness poor Molly couldn't understand her!

Will smiled as Molly stepped further away. "No wonder Dad drank his coffee black!" she said.

At the mention of their dad, Tommy suddenly stood up and rushed out of the barn. *Where's chatterbox off to?* I watched as he slumped over to the fields, wishing again that I could think of something to cheer him up. When I turned back to the barn, Molly and George looked uncomfortable, as though they knew Molly's words had upset their brother. But what were they meant to do? Never mention their dad again? That didn't seem right.

"OK, let's move on to cleaning hooves," Will suggested, cutting through the silence.

Molly was soon scraping a pointy peg-like thing into one of Nelly's hooves, but George seemed to have got bored of farming and sat in the corner of the barn playing on his games console.

Molly turned to Will. "I knew I could do this country stuff," she said with a smile. "It's just like having a pedicure really."

"You're a natural," Will agreed.

George looked up for a split second. "Yeah, right."

Molly ignored him and continued scraping. "In a former life I must have sat around on stone walls, picking apples from orchards and ... "

Nelly giggled. *What's so funny?* I wondered. Then I realised. She was ticklish!

But Molly hadn't noticed. " ... and riding horses across fields ... " she continued. Uh-oh – what could I do to warn her?

Nelly shook her head. "Hee ... bree ... hee!" she chuckled.

"... and I probably wore wellies and overalls and—"

"Hee-hee-breeeeee-heee!" Nelly suddenly shuddered. Then she gave a massive snort of laughter and kicked out a hoof – right in the direction of Molly. "Ohhhhhhhhh!" the horse yelled.

Molly flew across the barn and crashed into a stack of hay.

"Molly!" Will shouted, running to her. I chased after him. Was she alright? No girl deserved a hoof in the face!

CHAPTER TWELVE

Will and George helped Molly to her feet and led her
to sit on a hay bale. I licked her fingers nervously as
Will inspected her face.

"It looks fine," he said, after a moment. "It's just a
bloody nose." He dug a hand into his pocket and
pulled out a bunch of tissues. Molly tipped her head
back and held the tissues to her nose. Despite the fall,
she was still wearing the blue feather hat – with the
tissues she looked even more ridiculous. Not that now
was the time to tell her that.

"Look, it's OK, Molly. Not everyone's cut owt for farhmwork," Will told her.

Molly brought her head back up and looked at Will. "I just don't understand what I was doing wrong."

Will glanced at her outfit. "OK, well, y'know for star'ers, maybe next time you could wear something a li'le more appropriate, y'know … " He trailed to a halt. I could tell he was trying to be kind, but the words were all coming out wrong.

Molly stared at Will. "What are you saying?"

Will's cheeks flushed pink. "Err … nothing. It's just that—"

She stood up from the hay bale, pulling back her shoulders. "Are you saying I look stupid?"

Well, I'm glad you've worked that out for yourself, Molly!

But Will looked horrified – his mouth was opening and closing like a goldfish. "No … I didn't … look … "

You're really not doing a good job with your words today, I wanted to tell him.

"Forget it!" Molly pushed past him and stormed out of the barn.

Will watched her go, clearly baffled. Most boys wouldn't even notice if they'd upset a girl. Perhaps he *did* like her . . .

"Girls, hey," said George, shaking his head as he got up to follow Molly.

Will stared at the floor and sighed.

"Bye, Will!" I called as I chased after George and Molly. Although I felt sorry for Will, I had more important matters to paw. I needed to make sure Molly was OK.

❧

Inside the house, George was standing at Molly's bedroom door. "Molly, are you OK?" he asked.

"I'm fine!" she shouted back. She didn't *sound* fine.

"Molly, it's me," I barked. "Can I come in?"

I smiled as Molly opened the door a crack so I could scoot through the gap. I knew she liked me.

"Don't worry, George," I called. "I'll make sure she's OK."

Molly sat in front of her dressing table mirror, scrubbing at her face with a cloth. At last – that terrible turquoise paint had disappeared from her eyelids. I sat quietly on her bedroom floor, watching (although not before checking for any chickens or hares in the wardrobe). She sighed at her reflection in the mirror, then jumped up and grabbed a bin bag from the bed. She tugged off the blue hat (finally!) and stuffed it into the rubbish bag. Then she swung open her wardrobe door. She began pulling her clothes off the hangers and chucking them into the bag too.

"Molly – what are you doing?" I barked. Most of the

clothes were old-fashioned, I noticed – big frilly skirts, flowery blouses, more odd-looking hats. But I knew how much she loved her outfits. Why was she doing this?

"I think that's everything," Molly said in a determined voice. She ran downstairs with the bin bag – I followed at her heels to find out what she was doing – and stuffed it into the big metal dustbin outside.

I stood up on hind legs and peered into the bin. It was a bit drastic of Molly to throw all her clothes out, wasn't it? I mean, Will hadn't meant for her to do that!

"I think I'm going to have to take these kids under my paw," I said to myself, as Molly disappeared back inside the house. They were all unhappy in their own way. Good job there was a dog around. But who should I help first?

I dropped back down to all fours, and spotted Tommy out in the fields, sitting next to a fallen tree trunk – a speck in the corner of the field (it's a good job I have 20/20 vision). *Right – chatterbox first*, I decided. He was the one worrying me most of all.

I found a red rubber ball in the yard and grabbed it in my mouth, then I raced towards Tommy, over the fields. As I got nearer, I slowed down. I didn't want to scare him off.

He sat cross-legged in front of the gnarled old tree trunk, head down, his shaggy hair almost covering his face completely. He was fiddling with something in his hands. I stepped forward for a closer look – it was his dad's watch. You know, the one he'd taken from the box before they'd moved?

I don't think he'd even noticed me, so I set the ball on the ground and nudged it to him with a paw. "Game of ball?" I barked. If I could get him to play with me, maybe he'd open up and tell me how he was feeling – or I could at least cheer him up for a while. Who doesn't enjoy playing with a ball? I could do it for hours!

But as the ball came to rest in the grass in front of him, he just looked up and stared at me, those large brown eyes still full of sadness. Then he went back to examining the watch.

"No? Come on, mate," I pleaded. "This is how it works. You pick it up and throw it, and I run and catch it. Repeat, ad infinitum."

Tommy glanced up again. Was he melting slightly?

"Come on, Tommy," I barked again. "It'll help to cheer you up." I gave him my tilted head, doggy-eyed look. "I'm begging!" He looked at me, but there was still no smile. OK, time for the big guns. I stood on my hind legs and got into the begging pose, my front legs raised, paws tilting down. "Please play ball with me, Tommy," I barked in a small, high-pitched voice.

Finally! I'd got his attention, I could tell – I needed to make the most of it. "How about some dancing?" I began spinning around and swaying from side to side. "I got the skills to play the bills!"

Tommy giggled.

"Hey, it's not meant to be funny," I told him. But at least I'd got him smiling! I spun one way and then the other, doing a quick-step in the long grass, my tongue poking out in concentration. "I'm a skilled professional, you know!"

I sat back for a rest, but Tommy was still smiling at me. "Oh, you want some more, do you?"

Here goes! I pushed myself up to the tiptoes of my hind legs and raised my front paws aloft. "There. Eat. My. Moves!" This time I did a couple of street-dance spins, then I fell to the ground and performed the Pudsey wave. (If you don't know it – although you should! – it's where I raise one paw and then the other, over and over again. All the humans love it.) To end, I did a long roll across the grass, waved a paw one last time, and lowered my head to the 'play dead' position.

Then I jumped up, to see Tommy's reaction. He was

grinning from ear to ear! It had worked! The watch had fallen into his lap, forgotten for now. George wasn't feeling sad about his dad at all anymore.

My belly rumbled. *Time for lunch now*, I reckoned. *I think I deserve it.* After that, I'd make a start on Molly.

I touched my nose to George's hand, then ran to the house and gobbled up the pigs' ears Gail had left for me in a bowl in the hallway (don't tell Ken!). Before I went upstairs to find Molly, I rescued the bin bag from the dustbin.

"Urgh, this is heavy!" I said to myself as I dragged it up the stairs with my mouth. I pulled it into Molly's room. "What have you got in here?" I barked as I set the bag down.

She frowned at me. "Why did you bring that back up here?"

"Cos I don't *really* think you wanna chuck it away!"

Molly laughed. I was really starting to wonder if she could understand Dog . . .

"The only thing dressing like that ever got me was a world of grief," she said through gritted teeth.

"At least you were being yourself. And I speak as someone who almost had to wear a pink tutu. And pink is soooo not my colour!" I watched to see what she'd do next. If she was really determined to dump the clothes, she'd drag them straight back downstairs again. But there the bag stayed, on her bedroom floor. She wasn't looking at it exactly, but she wasn't trying to throw it away either. *Another job well done*, I told myself, scampering away. I'd just leave Molly for a few moments; give her time to think about what she wanted to do. A good dog knows when to leave people alone, and I'm a good dog. Scrap that! I'm a *great* dog!

"Stupid dog," she said under her breath as she turned back to her dressing table.

I raced back to the doorway. "Hey, I heard that!" I barked. She looked over her shoulder and smiled. Ha!

She didn't think I was stupid, not really. In fact, I was certain she was pretty fond of me.

Downstairs, George was stabbing at the buttons on his games console, tilting it from left to right. *Is that all he ever does?* I wondered. There had to be more he could do with his free time! But before I could pester him to play with me instead, Gail walked in.

"Argh, that man! He's so horrible . . . not to mention strange," she began.

"What? Who?" George asked without looking up from his game.

"Thorne! You know, where I've been working all day?" She set down her bag on the worktop and flicked the switch of the kettle. "His house is really weird – covered in antiques and freaky statues. And when I arrived he was wearing a badger onesie!"

That does *sound weird.*

"Anyway, how's your afternoon been, love?" she asked George.

"Meh," he replied.

Gail shook her head. "I can't believe you'd rather stay inside playing that thing. We are in a beautiful part of the country, surrounded by space . . . "

"Wrong kind of space— Die you poxy!" He jabbed at the buttons yet again.

Gail sighed. "You could take Pudsey for a walk."

"Dog not need walk," he replied.

I beg to differ!

I ran to the table, grabbed my lead in my mouth, jumped up on to George's back and peered over his shoulder. At that moment, Tommy ran into the kitchen and appeared on George's other side.

"Actually, dog *do* need walk," I barked.

George looked around at us both. "Are you ganging up on me?"

I nodded. "Yep!"

"OK, OK." George paused his game. "I know when I'm outnumbered."

CHAPTER THIRTEEN

It was great to get Tommy outside. The fresh air, the blue sky, the birds, the ... kite?!

"Look, Tommy, there's a kite stuck in that tree!" I barked. We were in one of the big grassy fields, and I could see it lodged high in the branches. I raced towards the tree.

George and Tommy were right behind me. On closer inspection, it didn't look flyable – the worn beige fabric was covered in tears.

"It looks like it's been there for a looong time," said George. "Creepy."

As we reached the tree, something else took our attention: a circular stone wall, covered by a large sheet of wood.

George headed straight for it. "I wonder what's under here."

I waited patiently behind George and Tommy as they lifted the sheet of wood, my tail wagging.

"Agggghhhh," said George, straining to push it off. It crashed backwards and we all peered inside. The bricks went down as far as I could see. It looked like an old well!

"Is this a good idea, guys?" I barked. I wasn't sure we should be near this thing. I had heard stories of humans – and dogs – getting trapped down wells.

"Hello!" George shouted down.

Hello ... hello ... hello ... the well echoed.

"Helloo, my name is Satan," George said in a deep, evil-sounding voice. "I will eat your spleen ..."

But his words were drowned out by another

sound – the noise of crumbling brick. Tommy's body lurched forwards as part of the wall fell away beneath him. Before I could even lunge to grab hold of him, he slipped further forward and tipped over into the well.

"Tommy! Tommy – no!" yelled George, reaching out to grab his brother.

"Catch him, George!" I barked. *I knew this wasn't a good idea!*

George had caught Tommy's hand, but he was dangling by his fingertips inside the well.

"Hold on, Tommy!" I called, but George was struggling to keep a grip on his brother's hand. This was awful!

"Nooooo!" shouted George as Tommy's hand slipped out of his. Tommy disappeared into the deep, dark well, hitting the bottom with a splash.

George's face went as white as a snowy owl. "Tommy, are you OK?" he screamed into the gloom.

I peered inside, careful not to lean on the ancient wall too much. I could just about make out Tommy, splashing around in the darkness, his arms reaching out to the sides. It looked like he was trying to climb up, but it was too slippery. "Tommy, talk to me, buddy!" I turned to George. "We've got to do something! Call the police! Wait – call Lassie!"

George stared at the well, walking backwards, shaking his head. "I can't let him drown!"

"Tommy, hang in there!" I called. "George – what are we going to do?"

"I've found a rope!" George shouted from the edge of the field.

"Good work, George. Now throw it down!"

George couldn't talk Dog, obviously, but we were thinking the same thing. George ran to the well and flung the rope inside.

"Grab it!" I barked. "Hold tight – we'll pull you up!"

I could only hope that Tommy would understand what he had to do.

Thankfully, I saw Tommy flail his arms at the rope above his head, but – oh no. He couldn't hold on to it properly – it was too short.

George spun around, his face almost translucent with panic.

What should he do now? He needed a longer rope! Wait – what about … "George – my lead! Use my lead!" I barked, jumping up and nudging my snout against George's jacket pocket.

George quickly understood what I meant. "Good thinking, Pudsey!" He fumbled in his pocket for the lead.

"Hang on, Tommy. I've got an idea!" I called down the well as George unravelled my lead and tied it to the end of the rope. "Oh yes, that should reach him!" I said.

George chucked one end of the lead down. "Put

your foot in the leash," he told Tommy desperately, then held tightly on to his end of the rope.

I jumped down from the well wall. "George, I can help!" I ran around behind him and grabbed the end of the rope with my mouth. "OK, ready when you are, George. Pull!"

George and I both grimaced as we pulled back on the rope. "Agh, ahhh!" we groaned. Boy, for a little kid, Tommy was heavy!

I dropped the rope for a second. "Hang on a minute," I said to Tommy, "I've got to get a better grip." I wrapped it around my legs, then put it back in my mouth. *That's better.*

"PULL!" shouted George.

I heard a splash – but a little one, not big enough to be Tommy falling back down.

"Leave it!" said George.

Uh-oh – was it their dad's watch?

"Tommy, just leave it!" I agreed. I knew it was

special to Tommy, but saving him was more important. "OK – now pull ... PULL!" I barked. Like a
tug-of-war, I strained backwards. "We can do it!" I
called to George. I could see his arms and legs shaking
as he used all his strength on the rope.

Then I saw the top of Tommy's shaggy-haired
head!

"Come on – pull!" I cried.

Tommy reached up to the edge of the crumbling
well, and George let go of the rope and grabbed his
brother. He hauled him over the wall, and both of
them fell to the ground. George and Tommy leant
back against the well, panting.

"Pudsey, we did it!" George grinned, his arm
around Tommy.

"I know – what a team!" I barked with relief. Little
Tommy had nearly ... I mean, he could have ...

"That was wicked!" cried Tommy.

George turned to his brother, his eyes boggling like

a toad's in a fly pond. His mouth fell open. I have to admit, so did mine!

"Did he just say something?!" I barked. This was immense!

"We're back!" I called ahead as the three of us – covered in mud – entered the house. "And you're gonna wanna hear this!"

We found Gail in the living room, rummaging around some bookshelves.

"We had the *best* time," said Tommy, walking in and plonking himself down on the sofa.

"Did I say that the countryside is awesome?" added George.

What? He's certainly changed his tune!

"Has anyone seen my purse?" asked Gail, turning to look at us briefly, a frown on her face.

"Do you remember when she lost her keys," Tommy said to George, giggling, "and they were in the front door all along?"

George chuckled and nodded.

"Look at the state of you." Gail looked at us properly this time. "Go and have a shower."

What? A bit of muck is character-building!

"Oh, Mum!" Tommy and George said in unison.

"Don't 'Oh, Mum' me!" Gail replied. "Go and—" She suddenly broke off, spun around slowly and stared at Tommy.

"What?" he asked.

"Oh my goodness. Tommy!" She rushed over and sat down beside him, wrapping him in her arms. "Oh, Tommy, thank you. Thank you."

"Yep!" I barked. "Cat got his tongue, dog got it back again!"

"Not so tight – I still need to breathe!" squeaked Tommy as Gail squeezed him in a hug.

She broke off and held his grubby face in her hands. "Why now? Why choose now to speak?" she asked gently.

Tommy glanced down at me. "Well, there's five of us again," he explained matter-of-factly.

"Just as well I'm covered in fur, isn't it?" I said. "Or you'd see how hard I was blushing!"

"Is that Tommy's voice?" Molly asked from the hallway.

Gail squeezed Tommy again. "Come here, you. And you." She beckoned to Molly. "And you," she said, reaching out her arm to George at the other end of the sofa. She looked down at me. "And you – don't think you're getting out of this."

I leapt on to their laps, and they all stroked me at once. I was right in the middle of a group hug. *I never thought I'd say it, but a dog could get used to this!*

"We should get takeaway to celebrate," Molly suggested.

"Fish and chips," said George.

"Or *sausage* and chips," I suggested. *Mmmmmm . . . sausages . . .* I licked my lips.

"Only if I can find my purse," said Gail, a small frown returning. "I think I left it at Mr Thorne's . . . "

George and I got up from the sofa. "Leave that to us," I barked. "Right, George?"

"We'll go and find it," he announced. "After all, I *am* the man of the house. It's my job!" He pointed down at me. "Pudsey, activate your smell-o-tron."

"You mean my nose, right?" We made quite the comedy double act.

"Let's rolllllll." George strode out of the room and I followed at his heels. His games console sat abandoned on the coffee table. Just the way I liked it.

"Don't get any more mud on you," Gail called after us.

As if! There was no time right now for playing in the dirt – not when sausages and chips were within sniffing distance.

CHAPTER FOURTEEN

We stood outside Thorne's gigantic Georgian mansion, gazing up at it. Why did one person need so much house? George rapped on the heavy wooden front door. There was no answer. George sighed and turned to me.

"His car's not here," I barked.

"I guess he's not in," said George, his shoulders slumped. "There's no fish and chips for us tonight, bud."

I shook my head. "Oh, don't say that. I'm on a promise of battered sausage – and I'm not giving up that easily!" I ran across the drive and through a gap in the gate in the garden wall. I called back over my shoulder: "I bet you there's a back way in!"

"Pudsey, no!" shouted George, but it was too late. My mind was fixed on sausages.

Around the back, I spotted an open sash window. Perfect! I summoned my top-notch gymnastic skills yet again and leapt through. I was in!

Sausages and chips, sausages and chips, went around my head as I raced through a huge room filled with old furniture, boxes and piles of dusty papers. "Right, where's this purse?" *Sausages and chips, sausages and chips – keep your eyes on the prize!* I told myself. I had to be quick or George would start getting worried.

I stuck my snout under the sofa – no. I snuck beneath a drawing table – no. I peered under a rug – still no. What's more, everything smelt like cat in there! *Urgh.*

Sausages and chips, sausages and chips ... Let's look

up here. I stretched up on my hind legs to investigate a side table – nope. *But wait – what's that?* At the other side of the room was a desk. I scampered over and jumped right on top. Gail's purse sat between a half-drunk mug of tea and a lamp in the shape of a mermaid. "There you are – gotcha!" *Sausages and chips, sausages and chips* ... I could almost taste them now.

I was about to leap down from the desk with the purse when I noticed something strange in the corner of the room. "What's that over there?" A weird mystical blue light shone out from behind a half-open door, like the ghost of a Georgian lord of the manor might be hiding in there. (OK, so perhaps I had been watching too many episodes of *Most Haunted* lately, but still – it was strange.)

Or ... maybe ... it was a fridge! Yes, that would be more like it! "It can't hurt to have a look," I told myself. "Thorne's got a few quid. I bet it's stuffed full of steak ... and pork chops ... and bacon ..."

I darted through the door, then stopped in my tracks. This wasn't what I'd been expecting. Inside was a huge table that almost filled the entire room. "Well, this isn't a fridge!" I reached up to the edge with my front paws to take a look. It was a miniature model countryside, covered mainly in grass fields with a few houses dotted about. I peered closer at a big country hall. "That's this place!" I realised. My gaze drifted left, to the centre of the table, where there was a cluster of buildings around a yard. "And there's home!"

Huh! I thought. *I just called it home! I've never had a home before!* I couldn't help but smile. *Blimey – how things have changed.*

I shuffled around the table of miniature Chuffington on my hind legs. "Oh, there's the village." A few houses and the pub surrounded the little village green. But the telephone box and the pie shop were missing. "Could have done a better village – that's rubbish!" I continued sidestepping, towards the corner of the table. My front paw landed on something which vibrated as I touched it. Suddenly, there came a whirring noise ... and the centre of the model countryside dropped away!

"What the ... ?" I heard more whirring and clicking and the crunch of mechanics. I watched the table carefully. The centre began to rise back up again – but it looked completely different to before! A huge white building with three tall storeys towered there now, stretching across the width of the miniature Chuffington. It was surrounded by car parks and motorway roads. Alarm bells began ringing like cowbells in my head – it looked like a ginormous shopping mall. And the farm – including Tumbledown Cottage – was nowhere to be seen!

"What *is* Thorne up to?" Panicky thoughts raced through my head: *Is Thorne going to destroy the farm? What will we do? Does anyone else know about it? Why would we want a mall around here anyway? I bet they wouldn't let dogs in – they never do! Would they sell sausages?*

The urgent ring of a phone broke into my thoughts and I swung around. *Uh-oh!* It was right here, in this very room, shaking in its cradle on a desk in the corner.

"Why must the phone always ring when I'm about to sit down to eat?" came a posh, grumpy voice from the hallway.

Oh no – Thorne's coming! What am I going to do?

"All right, all right, keep your hair on!" called the voice again, sounding nearer. I could hear footsteps.

I looked around the room for a hiding place. *Here goes nothing!* I thought as I disappeared out of sight.

"Yes, yes, I'm coming!" I heard someone enter the room, then, "Hello, yes, Thorne here." He picked up the phone. "Who is this?" his voice turned even more grumpy. "Ah, foreman! What? Look, we've been through this already. Season's End Farm is abandoned and derelict – and furthermore, it is a danger to the public. I want it razed to the ground, not one brick left standing on another."

What?! He was going to destroy the farm? Crouching in my hiding place, I shook with fury, but kept my mouth clamped shut – I couldn't risk letting out a bark.

"Yes, yes, yes," Thorne was saying. "All the paperwork has been submitted to the relevant authorities. You have my word on that. Oh, and one thing. On the day in question, gather your men together, but remain out of sight until I give the word ... Never mind why! But do this to my satisfaction and you may find a lot more work coming your way. A very great deal more. Do I make myself clear?"

I heard a clunk and the whirring noise started up again. Oh dear. There was nothing I could do as I felt myself rising upwards ...

"Boy! Now this is how to make an entrance!" I

joked, as I appeared in the room atop the mall in the centre of Chuffington village. Thorne's beady eyes almost popped out of his head when he saw me and his face turned a distinctly purple shade of beetroot.

"I'll call you back," he said into the mouthpiece, then slammed the phone down. "It's you!"

"Duh! Yes, it's me! Who else?"

He brought his furious face closer to mine. But I wasn't scared – I stayed right where I was. (Although I have to admit, the replica mall wasn't the comfiest dog seat in the world.)

"You fiend!" he yelled. "Not content with scaring off my beloved Faustus, now I find you here, sitting astride my future." He pulled out a tie from his pocket and wrapped it around his hands. "You leave me no choice ..."

"Oh wow, you wanna play? Brilliant!" I leapt off the table, scampering around the room as Thorne ran after me.

"Come here!" his voice rang out.

"Come on, Thorney-baby, try and catch me!" I wove around his legs in a figure of eight. This was the best chasing I'd had for ages.

"WILL YOU HOLD STILL!" Thorne yelled.

"This *is* fun – I love being chased!" I jumped up on a desk, running across the polished wooden top and brushing against a glass lamp which crashed to the floor. *Oops.*

"No, not that! That was Nanny's!"

I dived back down again and raced out of the door, knocking over an ugly statue of a horse with a human head. I winced as it shattered into a thousand pieces.

"Noooo!" Thorne screamed. "That's worth over a million pounds!"

But I was having too much fun to stop. "Can't catch me!" I cried. "Come on, tubby, keep up!"

CHAPTER FIFTEEN

"I'm sorry, Gail, but it states very clearly in your lease: 'No dogs'!" Thorne said firmly. "So I've arranged to have your ... *animal* sent away."

What?!

In the hallway of Tumbledown Cottage, I wriggled in the itchy lead that was strangling my neck. At the end of this lead was a grim-faced bald man. He was a member of staff at Thorne's country estate, who had eventually helped to catch me (only after I'd eaten all the truffles in the kitchen and ran upstairs for a good roll on the 400-thread-count

Egyptian-cotton bed linen — wow those sheets were *soft*).

Beside me and Baldy stood Thorne. Opposite us, Gail had her arms around Molly and George. I wondered where Tommy was.

"Sent away where? Why?" asked Molly. She was dressed in farm-girl-type clothes — a woolly patterned cardigan and billowy trousers, with a basket on her arm. I guessed this new image was for Will's benefit. I still wasn't sure he'd like it.

"Temporary retraining," replied Thorne with a smirking smile. "Don't worry, he'll be quite comfortable."

"What's the place called?" asked George. He sounded resigned. *No, George, I don't want to go anywhere! Don't let him send me away!*

"Um ... Dogs," said Thorne, his face colouring.

George frowned at him.

"Doggy-Dogs ... " Thorne paused and Baldy

nodded, although the dog-catcher still hadn't actually said a word. " ... erm ... Place," Thorne finished.

Huh – if that's a real place I'll eat my tail!

"Dogs Doggy-Dogs Place?" Molly twisted her face as she spoke. She clearly didn't believe it really existed either.

"Yes!" Thorne said in a high-pitched voice.

"He's lying – I can smell it!" I barked. "He's sending me away for ever!"

Molly and George looked at their mum. "Do we have a choice?" Gail asked.

"I'm telling you," I continued, "he's up to no good! Oh, why don't humans ever listen to me? I'm not just some dumb animal. I've seen what he's planning!" I felt so panicked, my heartbeat like a dragonfly's wings on a stormy day. I couldn't be sent away – not now, when I had to save the farm! "I wish you could all understand me ... I wish you could hear what I was saying ... I mean the farm is in danger, and you never know what— Oh look, sausages!"

Baldy dangled a string of juicy Cumberlands right under my nose. How could I resist those? He threw them out of the front door and I sprinted after them. *Sausages ... sausages ... delicious ... yum, yum, yum ...* I knew it was stupid, but all I could think about right then was getting my snout around those tasty, delicious meat treats. I followed my nose and found myself leaping into the back of a van. The sausages lay in the corner, calling out at me to scoff every last one of them – immediately!

But when I went to wrap my jaws around them, they squeaked. *Pudsey, you idiot!* They weren't real – these were toy sausages! I was so angry with myself – to be tricked so easily. I turned to run back out but Baldy the evil dog-catcher was standing at the doors, blocking my way. "Oh no!" I barked. He just grinned and slammed the van doors shut.

I leapt up at the rear windows, looking longingly at George as he ran out of the house to see me being kid-napped – or should I say *dog*napped?

"George!" I yelped.

"Pudsey!" He stood in the yard with big, sad eyes – just like his brother's, only George's were blue – as Baldy started the engine and the van rumbled away.

I stayed with my nose pressed up against the window as we moved down the drive, hoping George would do something to save me. But what could he do? The others were all inside with no idea what was happening. His silhouette became smaller and smaller as I kept watching, wondering whether I would ever see this family – *my* family – again.

I didn't move from that window as the van drove along lanes, roads and motorways – not once, not even when I was convinced I could smell a sausage roll being eaten by Baldy in the cab of the van. I figured that if I remembered which way we'd travelled, I'd be able to find my way back to the farm if I ever got a chance to escape. And I had to escape ... I had to save our home – the farm – from Thorne's destruction.

It was dark by the time the van turned into a huge gravelled area, lit by floodlights. It looked a bit like a quarry (I'd once been on a daytrip to Portland Quarry – don't bother, it's just a huge hole and piles of rocks, and they won't even let you help them dig), but it also had high walls and fences topped with barbed wire, with little rotating cameras mounted up on every corner. *This* was where I was being taken? I heard Baldy fumble at the van doors and I jumped out as soon as he threw them open – but he still managed to grab my lead and yank me back. Clearly, I wasn't going to escape that easily. I realised I would have to be clever about this, so I followed him obediently along the stone-covered ground and through a great metal gate. It crash-slammed behind us. I shuddered, and hoped that wasn't the last I'd ever see of the outside world. I wasn't ready to be a prisoner – I had my whole life ahead of me, with all my dreams still to fulfil. And I had to save the farm!

As Baldy led me down a dark tunnel, the howling and barking of hundreds of dogs behind the cell doors rang out, creating a terrible dog-prisoner orchestra. They all sounded so delirious I couldn't understand any words.

We reached a cell with an open door, and Baldy pushed me in. "Hey, no need for violence!" I said as I skittered inside. In the gloom I could make out a tiny tiled room with a cold, damp floor. I ran to the back, checking out the furniture. Nothing. "Where's my bed?" I barked.

The door banged shut, making the floor shudder for a moment and sending the cell into almost pitch blackness. *Not again!* I sank down on the dirty tiles. *And I thought the barn was bad!* I really was in a pickle now. How would I get out of this one? For the second time that day, I wished that somehow Lassie would come to the rescue. *Ah, Lassie, what would you do in a situation like this?*

CHAPTER 16

Somehow, on those freezing tiles that smelt of a thousand different dogs' pee, I did manage some sleep that night. But it was full of vivid dreams – actually, more like nightmares – of the Wilson family and the farm.

I dreamt of Tommy, back to being silent again. He lay on his bed with those terribly sad, lonely eyes.

When his mum came in, Tommy didn't even look up at her. "Dinner's nearly ready," she said quietly. "Pudsey will be back soon – you heard what Mr Thorne said." Gail's eyes filled with tears. "Well, you know where we are." She left the room and closed the door. Tommy hadn't moved a muscle. He seemed even worse than before. What had I done? All for the thought of sausages!

My dream blurred and switched to Ken in the yard. "'Ere, I just heard Jack and Gail talking," he said to Edward, who stood in his stable. "Pudsey's been sent away!"

Edward stuck his head out of the stable door and frowned deeply. "Sent away!" Edward sounded horrified. "Where?"

Ken shook his head. "Causing trouble, so they said. I'm gonna miss 'im ... " *I didn't know Ken liked me that much!*

"I've got a bad feeling about this, Ken," said Edward. "The sort of feeling I get before a big storm."

Ken began snuffling some hay up from the ground. "Oh, 'ere's how you get rid of *that* feeling! Huuuooohh ... " Ken took a deep breath. *Parrrrrrppp!*

came the noise from his backside. "Oh, yes!" Ken said with a grin.

"Ken, no – stop!"

Arrrrrrrppppp! the fart went on. "Sorry, Edward, can't put the genie back in the bottle. Oooohhh ... " *Aarrrrrrooooooopppppp.*

Yuck! It had been nice to see the animals missing me, but why did I have to dream about this?

Edward closed his eyes in disgust. "Please, do you have to?!"

Ken began walking away, his fart finally finished. "Sorry," he grunted.

The dream cut to Gail, sitting in Thorne's study holding some papers. She had a line between her eyes, as if she'd been constantly frowning. She turned to the computer and peered over the screen, looking like she was checking no one was about. She bit her lip and began typing on the keyboard.

'Dogs Doggy-Dogs Place' she wrote into the search

bar. Brilliant – she was trying to find me! Well, at least in my dream she was ... but it was so vivid I started to wonder if it was real. I don't think I've mentioned it before, but sometimes it seems as if I can delve into humans' minds – when they subconsciously want me to, that is. It never normally happens when it's helpful, like when I want to know exactly when the butcher's going to throw out his offcuts. But was it happening now?

The computer flashed up: 'Your search failed to find any results'. Of course it would say that – I was sure that this disgusting hovel wasn't really called 'Dogs Doggy-Dogs Place'. Thorne had just made up the name on the spot!

Gail sighed, took a sip of her tea, leant back in her chair and jumped – Thorne was sat right beside her!

"You seem agitated, Gail," he remarked in an even smarmier voice than usual (if that was possible). "Why don't you go home? You could bake some cakes for the fete tomorrow ..."

"Yes," said Gail, without even turning to look at Thorne. "Yes, yes – fine, OK."

She picked up her bag and walked out, and Thorne squinted at the computer screen.

Oh no – now Gail would be in trouble if Thorne knew she was looking for me. *Gail, Gail!* I called in my dream, but of course she couldn't hear me.

I heard a sudden gurgling sound. I shook my head and blinked my eyes. Sloshing. Then a gurgle. Then a slosh. This wasn't my dream – this was real. For a moment I had no idea where I was, but when I looked around at the titchy cell, it all came flooding back to me like the stab of a hepatitis jab.

Where's that slurp-gurgling coming from? I wondered. As the cell was pretty much empty, I soon found the source – a pipe that dropped down from the ceiling and ended just above the floor. Underneath it stood an empty bowl. I sniffed the air. This was food arriving, I thought, but if the smell was anything to go by, I wasn't sure it was edible! Sure enough, thick brown sludge began dribbling from the pipe into the bowl.

"Eurgh – disgusting! I'm not eating that!" Not that I was hungry anyway – I was way too anxious to eat. *Maybe I could go on hunger strike*, I wondered. *That works for human prisoners, doesn't it?*

I heard a Scottish bark from the cell next door. Then another, and another. *Is that dog singing?*

"Oh ye'll teke the high road and I'll teke the low road ... " Yep – he was definitely singing! What was there to sing about in here?

"Hello! Who are you?" I barked, desperate for some conversation after a lonely night. And maybe he could help give me some pointers to get out of here. "I'm Pudsey!"

"I'm Finnington Finbar Finnington Lachland McDonald Furgeson Fitzweasel McFudgebucket the Third," he barked chirpily.

"Oh yeah?" That was the most impressive name I think I'd ever heard. I wondered if I could add some more words to mine: *Pudsey mega-dog the brave, lord of Tumbledown and king of sausages . . .*

"But you can call me Finn!" my neighbour added. "I'm the head of the escape committee."

My ears pricked up. "You've got an escape committee? That's great! Who's in it?"

"Well, there's me and . . . erm . . . well actually it's just me!"

"So how do you plan to escape?" I asked. "I want in on it!"

"Well, there's only a wee problem there, Pudsey. The escape committee has done extensive research of the prison, and we've come to the conclusion . . ."

"Yeah?" I said.

". . . that it's impossible to escape."

I frowned. "So what's the point of having an escape committee then?"

"To *escape*, ye donut!"

"Eugh," I said to myself, laying back down. This escape committee had serious issues. "I'm gonna have to figure my own way out."

Something clicked, and I looked up. The door to my cell was slowly lifting.

"It's walkies," Finn explained. I could hear other doors opening in the building. They must have been letting all the dogs out. "Time for some fresh air – although don't ye expect green grass or a ball to chase. Come on."

Right, this is my chance to get back to the farm and warn everybody, I thought as I wandered out of the cell on to hard pebbly ground, the barks and howls of dogs ringing out all around me like church bells. I couldn't believe how many dogs there were here – Labradors, Dalmatians, schnauzers, poodles and a few dogs who were a mix of everything. I shook my head, forcing myself to focus on the task to hand. *Time for*

Pudsey the brave to— The door to my cell slammed shut behind me and made me jump. *What ... oh! That gave me a shock!* I wasn't used to such harsh surroundings.

I looked around. All I could see were high metal fences, cameras, razor wire ... *I don't think I could jump that fence.* The 'walkies' area had the quarry rock on one side and high fences all around the other, with barbed wire covering the top and CCTV cameras on each fence post. I watched one for a moment, stood still, then ran to the right before darting suddenly to the left. The camera whirred as it changed direction. *OK, so the cameras follow our movements, too. Tricky.*

I could tell the other dogs were watching me, the newbie, but I didn't let it bother me – after all, as an actor, I was used to being looked at. It didn't faze me. In the corner of the yard stood a wooden building on stilts, with no windows but a door set into the front. That had to be the guard tower – Baldy must have the camera footage all feeding into there. *But what does the building remind me of . . . ?* It was familiar, but I couldn't place my paw on it for the moment.

Then it came to me: the gazebo on the film set! I replayed the memory of it crashing down, the director screaming at me, and being sacked from the movie. *"Get that dog out of here!"* Suddenly, I had an idea . . .

CHAPTER SEVENTEEN

"What ya doing?" Finn came and sat beside me as I stared at the guard tower. He looked exactly as I had imagined him – an old dog with scraggly white hair.

"Oh, hello, Finn. I'm trying to figure a way outta here," I told him.

"Well, then – you'll be needing the escape committee," he said, his eyes lighting up.

"Yeah, maybe . . ." What I really needed was something – or someone – to distract Baldy and his cameras. I turned to him. "Hey, Finn, do you dance?"

Finn shook his head. "No. But come and meet

Simon. He *loves* dancing dogs." Finn jumped up and began walking across the pebbled yard.

"OK – I'll be there in a sec." I tilted my head, concentrating properly, taking in the stilts of the guard tower again. They were dug into the ground, not far from the barbed wire fence – just a couple of metres or so. *I think this could work.*

I wandered over to Finn. He sat chatting to a group of dogs. He introduced me to the odd bunch – some pedigree (like Simon, the King Charles spaniel, and Sally, the chow chow) some mongrel (like Ally, who seemed to be a mix of pointer and beagle) and some just plain weird-looking (like Danny, the very-long-haired Lhasa apso).

"It can't be done," said Simon adamantly, when I told them I was planning to escape, and that they'd be welcome to join me if they wanted out of this rubble-hole.

"Of course it can," I argued. "All we have to do is

work as a team! We'll be so much stronger if we work together. I've got an amazing plan ... " I gave a slight nod to the guard tower, not wanting to draw Baldy's attention. "He hardly ever seems to come out of his watchtower. We need to distract him. We'll split up into two teams. A dancing team, and a digging team."

"Huhhhh? A dancing team?" barked Butch, the boxer dog.

Sally screwed up her nose at me. "But we're dogs. We don't dance."

"Oh, don't we?" I realised I was going to have to show these dogs just what I could do – and what they could do too, if they put their minds to it. I ran into a long criss-crossed-metal tube, preparing to put on a show.

And, cue the music! (Well, in my head, anyway ...) "Deeeeeeeee ... Dee, dee ... doooooooh ... "

"Go, Pudsey!" shouted Butch. At least someone believed in me already!

The song rang in my head. It was one of my favourites to dance to. "La, la, la, doo, doo, doo ..." I stood up on my hind legs, almost touching the top of the tube with my ears, and raised a paw – then another. I jumped forwards, I jumped backwards, I spun, and I moonwalked. The dogs were mes-merised!

I dropped to a crouch and quick-stepped along, did a handstand and then collapsed into the worm, bark-ing in time to my imagined song. By now, even Simon was nodding his head to my rhythm.

Time for the tail spin. Back on all fours I circled, pretending to chase my tail and completing a series of perfect spins. Then into more hind-leg jumping, this time with my paws aloft so I tapped the top of the tube each time. Wow. I'd forgotten just how much fun this was. I hadn't danced so hard for ages!

Now the dogs were swaying and raising their own paws as I danced. I did one last hind-leg-hop through the length of the tube, lifted both paws, and then dropped to the ground to signal the end of the show.

"Well, after that performance, I've changed my mind," said Simon, a serious look in his black eyes. "Pudsey, we'll help you escape. You're going to Chuffington!"

Sally suddenly yapped. "Everyone, scarper!" She nodded to the guard tower. "Look like dogs!"

I glanced up at the nearest camera. It faced right at me. *Uh-oh.* Had I been busted already? I hoped I hadn't ruined the surprise of my plan. The mechanics whirred as the camera moved around the rest of the yard. Maybe not. I beckoned the dogs into a corner of the walkies area, where it would look like we were just sniffing each other's bottoms (not that I like to do that, generally speaking – there's always a risk of somebody letting one go and being suffocated by a repugnant fart).

"OK, action stations. Ally, Rup and Jimmy –" (Rup was a German shepherd, Jimmy a husky) – "you take charge of all the big dogs. And Nicky, Lou and Danny –" (Nicky was a Jack Russell, Lou a Yorkshire terrier) – "you take charge of all the dancing dogs."

They nodded.

"Joey's in charge of switching cameras to distract Baldy and, Fuzzy-Cheeks – oh, nice to see you again!" I didn't expect to see *him* – although I guessed he must have got captured after being on the run from Mrs W. I wasn't sure what was worse – being bathed and primped by that big pink monstrosity or being imprisoned in here.

"Excuse me," barked Finn. "What about the head of the escape committee?"

"Oh, Finn, I forgot about you." I thought quickly. "Erm, how would you like to be promoted?"

Finn's brown eyes lit up. "To what?"

I thought quickly. "You can be chief of intelligence."

He beamed. "Oh, that's great!" Then he turned to Fuzzy-Cheeks and lowered his voice. "Erm ... what does that mean?"

"OK, Joey," I instructed the chihuahua. "Go and take control of the cameras."

Joey ran off to the control box I'd spotted on one of the guard tower stilts. He began pressing buttons with both front paws. Excellent – he looked like he knew what he was doing.

I pointed to the dancing dogs, gathered in a group on my left, at the front of which stood Nicky, Lou and Danny. "Jumping dogs, to your positions!" They scampered across the yard, centring themselves in view of the various cameras. "Get ready, Joey!"

Joey jabbed at the buttons and the cameras whirred. The dancing team began leaping up and down and barking, just like I'd shown them. Brilliant!

"OK, digging team!" I turned to Ally, Rup, Jimmy and their crew. "Let's dig like dogs!"

"Aye! What Pudsey said," barked Finn.

The bigger dogs raced to the stilts of the guard tower, two or three dogs around each stilt, and started scraping at the gravelled earth with their paws. *Dig, dig, dig* – the dogs dug into the stony ground like I'd never seen dogs dig before. It was incredible!

I stood in front of the tower, between the dancing dogs and digging dogs, directing. I checked on the dancing dogs – still jumping and spinning (some with real grace and panache – did I have some competition on my paws?) – then turned back to the dogs at the tower legs. Great big holes had appeared around each stilt. "Right, now use the cables to pull the front legs!" I told them.

The digging team stopped pawing the ground and clamped their teeth on the ropes that led from the guard tower. A bit like when we rescued Tommy from the well, this would be like one big tug-of-war. I just hoped us dogs were on the winning side!

Meanwhile, Joey still stabbed at the camera buttons, intent on ensuring old Baldy couldn't see the digging and toppling operation – all he would get in his cameras were the dancing dogs, strutting their stuff. I laughed as Nicky did a three-turn roll, and Pup the shih-tzu performed the worm. These dogs learned fast! *Work, it, yes, work it!* With any luck, Baldy would be mesmerised.

I turned back to the digging dogs, now dangling from the cables, pulling with all their might. Were they strong enough? Had the holes around the stilts been dug deep enough to make the tower unsteady? At first nothing budged, and the dogs barked and howled with frustration.

"Keep going!" I yelled to Jimmy, Rup and Ally, who raised their paws to summon up even more effort from their team, the ropes still clenched between their teeth.

The dogs yanked on the cables even harder – I

could see their legs shaking from the strain. Something creaked, and I looked up at the shuddering, wavering guard tower.

"Good job, guys! Now – stand back!" I yelled.

CHAPTER EIGHTEEN

I'd warned them all just in time – I didn't want any squashed dogs on my paws. Everyone raced away from the guard tower as it began tilting from front to back like a rocking horse. It creaked and shuddered, wobbled and tipped, the ropes snaking about on the ground below. But would it collapse completely? For my plan to work, it had to!

"Argggghhhh!" came a scream from inside. "What's going on?!"

All we could do was stand and watch – and I

crossed all my fingers and toes (not easy to do with paws!). *Come on, please! There's no other way!*

On the next screech, the two front legs of the tower broke away and crashed to the ground. "Yes!" I barked. Everyone around me began hopping up and down, waiting for what might happen next.

The guard tower swayed much more powerfully now, rocking on just two legs like a see-saw. It had to come down soon, but that was still no guarantee my plan would succeed – I needed it to tumble into the fence so we could escape! If it went the other way, into the quarry face, the high mental fences would stay intact, imprisoning us inside. We'd still be stuck here.

I gazed up as the tower swung back and forth, back and forth, screams from the guard ringing out from inside. "Help! What's happening? Arggghhh!" *That will teach him to fool me with toy sausages!* I thought.

Then – *BOOOOOOOM!* – the tower lurched one last time and crashed to the ground, kicking up plumes of white chalky smoke. The air was thick with it – I couldn't see a thing! But it began drifting to the floor and I blinked my eyes to clear them . . . *Yes! Oh, yes!* The tower lay on its side, the back stilts sticking out at angles. I could just see a set of arms and legs waving madly in the rubble. Baldy was starting to get to his feet, but the tower had crushed a large section of barbed-wire-topped fence to the ground. Enough space for even the biggest of Great Danes to fit through. We had our way out!

"Come on, let's go, let's go!" I felt like Indiana Jones. If only I'd had a fedora hat to look the part!

I leapt over the toppled fencing, hopping from paw to paw to avoid the barbed wire. I glanced over my shoulder to see all the other dogs following me, grinning from ear to ear, their tails wagging.

"Follow us!" shouted Finn as he jumped to freedom.

I didn't stop running for hours. There was no way I wanted to risk Baldy catching me. I figured all the other dogs had their own places to go – they didn't need me any more, and they soon dispersed, racing to their homes. I had to focus on saving the farm – so I thought back to the journey in the van and began tracing the same route home, just in reverse. Swing left, turn a sharp right ... I hoped I was going in the right direction but, as I think I've mentioned, my memory isn't the greatest. I ran along main roads at first, but eventually they changed into farmland lanes. Was I getting close?

"Oh, look!" I barked to myself. A signpost stood at the corner of a crossroads I was approaching. I put on the brakes and squinted up at the little letters. It read 'Chuffington: 1 mile'. I could have cried at that moment (although please don't mention that to anyone – I like to keep up the impression that I'm a brave, tough dog). I was almost home!

I turned into the lane that the sign pointed to. Well, actually, it was more of a dirt track. Was this the road Gail had bumped the car down when I was stuck inside the trailer? It had so many pot holes, I bet it was! Wow, that felt like months ago, I realised, when actually it had been just a few days. I sprinted along the track, swerving around the muddy puddles (normally I'd have been the first to splash in them, but today they'd have just slowed me down) and leaping over rocks and stones.

I rounded a bend in the lane and stopped in my tracks. "Oh no!" A large group of workmen stood in my path, chatting. They each held a mug of tea in one hand, and had a sledgehammer or axe in the other.

Looming up behind them were bright-yellow bulldozers and diggers. The farm had no chance against all this!

I'm too late, I said to myself. *Thorne's army are already here. I'm never gonna get past that lot.*

I crept backwards, away from the workmen – I didn't want them to spot me. "There can't be much time left," I said to myself. "And the fete will be starting soon – hadn't Mary said it was today? Everyone will be there. I'm the only one who can stop Thorne from destroying the farm!" But how could I do that if I couldn't even get near our home?

I stopped in a grassy patch at the side of the lane, out of sight of Thorne's army. I didn't want to get too far away. I lay down – I always find sprawling out helps me to concentrate. "I need to think ... Come on, Pudsey, think. Think, think, think."

"Hey, Pudsey!"

Huh? I would have recognised that Scottish accent anywhere – Finn!

I jumped up. "Finn! Where did you come from?" The lanky lurcher trotted down the lane towards me.

He crossed over to the clearing. "I thought I'd come and give you a hand," he chuckled. I didn't like to tell him that this wasn't a laughing matter.

I pulled a face. "You shouldn't have bothered. Thorne's about to demolish the farm. And there's *nothing* I can do about it."

Finn held up his paws. "Well, *I'm* here now, aren't I? And *you're* the one that said we're stronger together."

I shook my head. Finn didn't get it. "But they're blocking the way between us and the farm. And as I'm the only one that knows what Thorne's up to, they're bound to be looking out for dogs! He knows I'm clever enough to escape!"

Finn winked at me and raised one of his fluffy eyebrows. "Well ... then ... we'll make sure they don't *see* any dogs!" He glanced around. "Aha!"

What was he on about? "Finn?"

"I've got an idea, young Pudsey." He walked away from me towards a shed set back at the rear of the clearing.

"What? Where are you going?" I raced after him.

"Look at this!" he said, pulling at some fabric that hung up in the shed. "A beekeeper's outfit!"

"And ... ?" I asked.

With another tug the outfit fell to the floor. "And ... we can dress up in this. We'll disguise ourselves to get past those wee workmen!"

Has he finally lost it? I wondered. Mind you, after all that time cooped up in doggy prison, I wouldn't have been surprised.

I shook my head at Finn. "We can't fit into that!"

"Do ye wanne bet on it? Come on, don't be a spoil sport!"

CHAPTER NINETEEN

I never thought I'd say this, but minutes later I was inside a big white beekeeping jacket, standing straight on my hind legs. The jacket was more like a long dress really – it came down to below my knees. We just had to hope the workmen army didn't notice my fluffy legs poking out of the wellies!

I had Finn balanced on my shoulders, the top half of the beekeeper, with one of those funny, wide-brimmed hats on his head. The thick net that flowed from it meant no one would see his furry, doggy face. In each front paw he held a bunch of long twigs, which stuck out of the sleeves like fingers. I know, not very convincing – we were just hoping the workmen didn't look too closely!

How the mighty have fallen, I thought. This was pretty much as far away from a film set as I could get. Then I remembered that this was all for a good cause. A desperate one, in fact! I *had* to save the farm.

"OK, and we're off," I said through gritted teeth. I stepped forward slowly, Finn teetering on my shoulders. "Stay steady!" I called to him. It was like balancing a baboon on my back. His knobbly hind paws didn't help, driving into my shoulders.

"Uh, oh, uh," we both groaned together as the 'beekeeper' moved tentatively forward. The men with shovels hadn't noticed us so far – how would they react?

"Why ... uh ... am I ... uh ... on the bottom?" I complained. "You're bigger than me!"

"Be quiet," hissed Finn. "Ye're much bet'er at the two leg thing."

I didn't feel much better at that point – it was all I could do to stay up straight while holding such a weight. He might have been skinny, but Finn sure had heavy bones!

"Whoahhhh, steady!" he whispered, shuffling around on my shoulders.

"Get 'or 'aw 'ou of my 'outh!" I squealed. Eurgh. I'd have to chew Dog-Mint Dentals for days to get rid of the taste of Finn's hind paw.

"Sssssshhhhhhhh! Be quiet!" hissed Finn. "We're getting close to the workmen now."

I continued wobbling forwards. I couldn't see a thing through the jacket, and was relying on Finn to guide me. Would the men with shovels notice something strange about the figure passing them? I could hear them talking amongst themselves. The voices seemed to come to a halt as we kept walking – were they watching us? Hopefully, they were too busy planning the destruction of the farm to wonder why a juddering beekeeper with twigs for hands was walking past them *very* slowly.

"That's it!" Finn said quietly.

"What, really? We're through? We've done it!" I kept wobbling forwards in my wellies anyway, to be sure we'd got far past the army. I was one step closer to saving the farm! "Oh, Finn, I could kiss you!"

"Well I would'ne recommend it ... I was licking my bits earlier."

"Eughhhhhhhh."

Still, my heart felt like it was pumping out of my chest. Then – hold on. What was that noise? Was that the sound of engines starting up? "Finn, what's going on?" I cried.

"I don't know! Turn around so I can look behind us!"

I tottered around carefully. "Can you see anything?"

Silence. Then, Finn said, "Oh no, Pudsey, I think they're on the move!"

My heart sank to the tip of my tail. "Shoot – we're gonna be too late." *Now what?* I thought quickly. We couldn't face up to these men and their diggers on our own. "We need to get out of this ridiculous costume first."

"OK—whoah!" Finn cried, wobbling on my shoulders. I could feel the weight of his body moving forwards ... forwards ... Both of us yelled as the 'beekeeper' collapsed in a heap. I wriggled out from the jacket, which was still draped around Finn's shoulders – although he'd lost the hat. He didn't look as though he'd hurt himself, falling. He leapt quickly to his feet.

"You head for the farm ... " I told him, pointing a paw across the fields.

"OK!" he barked.

"... I'll go find Jack and get help."

"Riiiight – good luck!" He dashed off before I could tell him the same, his long legs taking him towards the farm house. He couldn't see the farm house, but I knew that his sense of direction would get him there. He'd found me, hadn't he?

I sprinted over the fields – although after my escape from prison earlier, I had no idea where I got the energy from, especially as I hadn't eaten since *yesterday*! I saw the fete in the distance – all the stalls set up on the village green, with bunting draped over lamp-posts and a stage at one end. It looked busy – like everyone from the village was there. I had to find Molly, or George, or Tommy, or Gail. I had to warn them. Thorne's diggers were headed towards their home!

CHAPTER TWENTY

Finally, I arrived at the fete. I ran on to the village green. *Oh, look, there's Peter with his giant pie – but no, I can't stop! Pie and gravy ... pie and gravy ... No! I must find the family. Where are they?*

The PA system suddenly screeched. I looked over – a guy in a dog collar (the white collar a vicar wears, although I must say it's very confusing that they're called that – as if humans are anything like dogs!) stood on the stage in front of a group of cub scouts.

"Well, it is lovely to see so many of you here, on this perfectly wonderful day for our annual village fete," began the vicar. "But I'm sure you'll all agree with me that Chuffington is more than just a mere village. We are a united community. And so I proudly declare, this grand fete ... OPEN!" He raised his hands in the air, and the villagers cheered and applauded. Everyone seemed to be in front of the stage – everyone apart from Jack, Gail, George, Tommy, Molly and Will. Where were they?!

I ran past the stage towards the area with stalls lined up alongside each other. *Oh, look, there's Peter and his giant pie ... Pie and gravy ... pie and gravy ...* I drooled like a newborn puppy, I wanted that pie so much – but I couldn't stop!

The next stall was a strongman game. I ducked as a giant of a man with a belly like a hippo's swung the hammer back. It was then that I heard a familiar voice. It was Will!

"Molly! You've changed your look again," he said.

Molly? Where is she? I peered through the crowds of

people. There she was, walking ahead of Will. He was right – she was back in the old-fashioned clothes, in a purple and lace frilly dress, and she had a crown of purple flowers in her hair. I thought they looked rather lovely, actually – much better than the blue hat.

"Molly!" I barked. "Wait for me, please – I need to speak to you!"

"This is the real me," I heard Molly telling Will without so much as glancing at him. "Just deal with it.

Will looked baffled – again. "I don't understand," he stuttered.

"Look, you only asked me out after I'd *changed*. If you can't handle me being a massive weirdo then . . . I don't want to go to the fete dance with you."

So Will had asked Molly to this evening's dance? That was huge! So why was she so angry?

Molly stomped away towards a stall. A coconut shy. *Oh, I wonder if they'll let me eat a coconut? I've never tried one of those! No, Pudsey,* I told myself. *I've got to*

186

concentrate on saving the farm – food can wait until later. But even though I kept barking, Molly hadn't noticed me. She grabbed a ball, frowned and flung it at a coconut as if it were the head of her enemy. It toppled to the ground. Bullseye! I remembered the boy on the bus back in London. Maybe she was imagining the coconut was him. Or maybe Will … She took another ball and launched it – bullseye again!

Will caught up to her. "Molly, please, what have I done?"

She continued flinging balls at coconuts as she spoke. "I'm not like you, Will. I won't change myself for a boy." *Throw … bullseye. Throw … bullseye.* Man, she was good!

"Then don't!" said Will. He frowned, looking utterly perplexed. "I liked you when I first met you. I never asked you to change."

"But you only asked me out when I tried to dress *appropriately*," she insisted.

"I asked you out when I saw you wearing that weird army get-up. That's how much I liked you."

Huh – what outfit was that? Had I missed one while I'd been in doggy prison?

Molly launched yet another coconut … but this one missed, and I noticed that her face had softened. Maybe Will had talked her round. I hoped so. They'd make a beautiful couple, like a leading lady and her leading man!

"Watch it, will ya!" A man popped up behind the coconuts, rubbing his head.

Molly looked mortified. "I'm sorry. I'm so sorry."

"Yeah, well," said the man, still looking pretty cross, "here's your prize. Well done." He passed Molly a fluffy brown teddy bear. It looked pretty soft and cuddly – although I would have preferred if it were a dog!

I have to get Molly's attention, I realised. She still thought I was in Dogs Doggy-Dog Place – no wonder she hadn't noticed my barking. There was nothing else for it.

I took a deep breath, sprinted up to Molly and leapt at her. As I've said before, I don't usually like throwing myself at people – but needs must and all that.

"Molly, Molly, quick!" I cried. "Jack's farm is in danger! You've got to come and help. You've got to come and help!"

Molly crashed backwards with me on her chest, right into the middle of Mary's cake stall. Cakes and muffins flew into the air.

"Sorry, sorry!" I barked. "Sorry, Molly!"

Will grabbed Molly's hands to pull her up. "Are you OK?"

While Will checked that Molly was all right, I noticed Jack walking on to the village green. "Jack, Jack!" I ran off towards him desperately.

"Something's wrong," said Will behind me.

Yes, something is *wrong – will somebody please listen to me?!*

I pawed at Jack's legs. "What is it, boy?" he asked.

"Jack, you've gotta come with me!" I barked.

George appeared beside him. *George!*

"I think he wants you to follow him," George said.

"Yeah, duh – of course I want you to follow me!" I barked. But secretly, I was just relieved someone had understood me. I knew I could rely on George!

Jack pointed at his truck. "Get in the back!" George, Molly, Will and Jack ran over to the truck and I began sprinting along the lane towards the farm. I heard the engine start and didn't look back. They'd follow me now, I was sure of it.

I raced across the fields until I got to the top of the hill that looked out over the cottage. Jack and his truck kept up behind me. Finally, we crested a hill. At the other side, the workmen, bulldozers and diggers formed a procession, marching down the hill – right

190

towards the cottage. They really did look like soldiers going to war. Perhaps in Thorne's eyes they were.

I heard Jack's truck pull up behind me. "There!" I barked. "Look!"

Jack yanked on the handbrake and everyone piled out.

"What's that all about?" asked Molly as she took in the army of workmen and their vehicles.

"Is that Thorne's car?" said George.

What? I hadn't spotted that, but George was right – Thorne's Range Rover (the windscreen still edged with red paint) trundled along beside the bulldozers. *He must be making sure they obey his orders!*

Molly squinted into the distance. "Yeah, it is. And they seem to be heading to your farm, Jack!"

Jack slouched against the bonnet of his truck, staring out at Thorne. "So he's finally doing it," he said quietly.

We all turned to look at him. What did he mean?

"What's he up to?" asked Will.

Jack stuck out his chin. "Something's 'e's wanted to do for a long time."

"Yeah, ruin the village!" I barked. "And I've seen the plans!"

Molly glanced back at the army, then returned her gaze to Jack. "What should we do?"

"Go warn the villagers," said Jack. "This affects them too." He jumped into the truck again. "I'll go and see if I can talk some sense into my brother."

"What?!" I barked, looking round at Molly and George – their mouths gaped open, just like mine. Thorne was his *brother*?

CHAPTER TWENTY-ONE

Before I knew it, we were back at the fete, panting. (We'd sprinted all the way – honestly, I'd never done so much running in all my life!) We ran from stall to stall and found Gail dropping off boxes of cakes at Mary's stand. At least these ones hadn't been ruined.

"Mum!" yelled Molly.

Gail spun around and looked down at me. "Hey, how is Pudsey here?"

"Umm . . ." George and Molly followed her gaze. I suddenly realised they hadn't been surprised to see me at all! Clearly I was such a mega-dog, escaping from prison is something they expected me to do – no questions asked.

Meanwhile Will ran on to the stage and grabbed the microphone. I winced as it screeched again.

"Everyone," he bellowed into it. "We need yer help!" He broke off to pant, still recovering from the run here. "Thorne's gonna destroy Season's End Farm! We 'ave to stop 'im!"

Will turned as the vicar tapped him on the shoulder. "Young man, young man," he said.

"We 'ave to stop him! Listen to me!"

"Young man, please, get down from there!"

"But, reverend, reverend—" Jack held out his hands to the vicar.

"Get DOWN from here, young man!"

Will shook his head and jumped off the stage.

"What is going on?" Gail asked Molly and George.

But Molly didn't answer. She stared around at the fete. "Where's Tommy?" she asked, her voice suddenly very high.

"He's still at the farm," said Gail.

"He's still at the farm?" I barked. "Oh no!"

George grabbed his mum's arm. "But they're gonna demolish the farm!"

"What?!" Gail's face had turned white.

"I told you Thorne couldn't be trusted," I said. "There's something really weird about him!"

"Thorne is a *nutjob*!" Molly told her mum, her eyes dark with anger.

"OK, let's get in the car. Come on, Puds!" Gail ran over to their car, and Molly, George, Will and I followed. I sat on Molly's lap in the front seat (I get car sick if I sit in the back).

"Let's go!" I barked as Gail started the engine. She drove the car around the back of Peter's pie stall, but there was one big problem: cars were parked bumper to bumper on the road beside the village green. "Oh, no, this way's blocked!"

Gail slammed down her hands on the steering wheel. "Argh!"

"Back up, back up," said Will.

But reversing between the fete's stalls would take ages. "I can't wait!" I told them, and I leapt out of the open window (with a perfect crouched landing, even if I do say so myself). "I've got to get to Tommy!" If he was anywhere near the farm, he was in serious danger!

I glanced over my shoulder to see Gail reversing into the back of Peter's pie stall. The car bumper nudged Peter, who went flying into the table of pies – landing smack on top of the giant one. Delicious meaty chunks in gravy came spilling out. *Oh, if only I didn't have an emergency on my paws! Pie and gravy . . . pie and gravy . . .* But there was no time for me to take advantage of the spilled pie.

"Sorry, Peter!" I heard Molly shout out.

I raced over the fields, my mind firmly set on Tommy, not letting any more thoughts of pie and gravy distract me. I'd seen those bulldozers – they could easily crush a little boy like Tommy. He'd have no chance!

I reached the top of the hill and saw Jack in his truck. He was driving up behind Thorne and his army – who were still marching towards the farm.

"There's nothing you can do, Jack!" Thorne shouted as he spotted his brother in the truck beside him. "You are too late!"

"This is madness!" said Jack over the sound of the engines. "You're gonna destroy everything we've ever known!"

"Who cares about that? This is my land, and the only thing in my way is your farm."

"But it belongs to the family!" Jack's face had turned almost as red as Thorne's. "*Our* family!" he yelled, shaking his head. "There must be another way that we can set'le this."

"This is the only way I can return Chuffington Hall to its former glory," Thorne said.

What was he talking about – a shopping mall wouldn't bring it glory! Just annoying customers!

"Who cares about the hall?" said Jack. "We were never really happy there anyway!" Jack stared at Thorne, his eyes locked on his brother's. "Come on. Why don't you come and live with me on my farm?"

"Oh, please," Thorne chuckled. "I have my standards, you know!"

I shook my head. It was clear Jack would never make Thorne see reason. The army of workers trundled onwards, now just metres away from the cottage. If the army wasn't going to stop, I had to get to Tommy.

I sprinted down the field. "Tommy, Tommy!" I yelled. *Where is he?* I saw a movement in an upstairs window of the cottage. I squinted as I ran – yes, it was Tommy, I would recognise that shaggy hair anywhere.

"Tommy, get out of there!" I shrieked. But he'd disappeared from the window. Had he heard me barking? Had he seen the bulldozers and ran out of the cottage to safety? I could only hope so.

I looked back – one of the diggers raced ahead of the others. What was happening? Had Thorne sent it ahead? It was then that I noticed no one in the driver's seat. *A runaway? Oh no!*

The digger jugged along the field, building speed as it travelled downhill. If Tommy was still in the house then this could be a disaster. What had Thorne done?!

I ran towards the cottage, and saw Tommy coming out of the front door – thank dogness! "Tommy!" I barked. "Get away from the house!"

But he couldn't have heard me over the digger engine, and instead of running away, he raced in front of the house and stopped right in the path of the runaway digger!

"No! No!" shouted Tommy, standing and waving

his arms. He hadn't realised no one was driving it! "NOOOOO!" he screamed.

I sprinted towards him. The digger rushed onwards, breaking through the fence in front of the house like a doggy tongue through gravy. If the digger did that to wood, what would it do to Tommy?

"Tommmmmmmmmmmy!" I yelled, my legs hammering the ground like a dog-lympian's as I raced to reach him. "Tommmmmmmmmmmyyyyyyy!"

CHAPTER TWENTY-TWO

With the digger just metres away, I launched myself at Tommy and threw him sideways on to the ground. My fur ruffled as the machine roared past us, smashing into the living room window of the cottage. All I could hear was the sound of glass shattering and bricks crunching as I lay on the grass beside Tommy. Then all was silent. I looked up and saw the digger half inside the house, half outside, its huge wheels butted up against the brick wall of the living room.

I suddenly realised Tommy wasn't moving at all. I nudged him gently with a paw. Nothing! "Tommy!" I barked. "Tommy, wake up!" I licked his face. He didn't move. *Oh no!*

I heard a car door slam. Was this help arriving?

"Good stuff!" said a posh voice from the other side of the digger.

Thorne?! Is he really so evil he'd be happy that he's hurt a child?

"Excellent, well done!" he continued, then: "What's the matter? Why have you stopped?"

"Look what it did!" said a gruff workman's voice.

Jack came running over. "That's enough! You've gotta stop this NOW!" he bellowed at Thorne. When his brother didn't reply, Jack rushed towards Tommy and me.

"I can't wake him up!" I barked at Jack. He knelt down beside Tommy.

"Well, don't just stand there," Thorne screamed at the workmen. "Keep going! We've got work to do – I want this whole site cleared."

Jack turned Tommy over into the recovery position (*Well done, Jack!*) just as Gail's car screeched to a halt beside the cottage.

"What did you do to my brother?" shouted Molly as she, Gail, George and Will ran towards us.

"He won't wake up, Molly," I explained. They all gathered round and Gail took Tommy's head in her hands. Her face was white.

"Tommy, it's Mummy," she said gently.

I could barely hear her over Thorne. Unbelievably, he was still ranting. "I ordered you – now smash down this farm!"

Will turned round to him. "If you wanna smash down this farm, yer gonna 'ave to go through us!"

Thorne held out his hands, as if he was being totally reasonable. "I'm replacing this *eyesore*," he said calmly, "with something you'll all benefit from, you idiots."

What? Did he really think we wanted a shopping mall here instead of our cottage – our home?

"Tommy, it's Mummy," Gail repeated.

"A magnificent, modern, state-of-the-art shopping mall. There'll be cafes and restaurants and –" Thorne held up a finger – "ample parking!"

"Oh, shut up, you awful man," Gail spat. "Somebody call an ambulance!"

Thorne looked down and his eyes widened. He took a step back, seeing what had happened for the first time. Had he been so focused on his army and his ranting that he'd not realised Tommy was hurt?

"THIS IS ALL YOUR FAULT!" I growled.

Thorne staggered backwards. I kept barking. I was so angry right then – how could Thorne have done such a terrible thing? He should be the one in prison!

Thorne slumped back against the digger as I continued to bark and growl. His eyes rolled into the back of his head and he slid towards the ground. He was so terrified of me he'd collapsed!

"Pudsey," came a voice.

I spun around. "Tommy!"

He'd opened his eyes – and he was smiling.

"You're awake! Hey, buddy!" I'd never been so glad to hear a human talk in my life. I rushed over to him and rubbed my head against his chin. "You've been asleep for ages," I explained. "You didn't wake up. I tried to wake you up ... I was trying to be a hero ... but then I wasn't really a hero cos ... " I drifted off – I was rambling. I turned to Thorne. "What is it with you, Thorne. Why don't you like dogs?"

Thorne's eyes were still rolling as he lolled against the digger. I stared at his face as he seemed to pass out into a dream. And at that moment – call it my own doggy sixth sense – I could see into his mind as he slept.

"He's perfect, he's perfect," said a man in a red velvet dressing gown. He looked like Thorne, except he had a moustache, and he held a tiny brown Labrador puppy. He kissed its head as he spoke.

A boy in pyjamas sat cross-legged on the floor in front of a fire. "Stupid dog," he said with a frown.

Hang on, where are we? I thought. What *was* this dream?

"So you don't like my puppy, huh?" the older man asked, raising an eyebrow. Next to him stood a women in a flowery dress with an ugly scowl on her face.

Is that your mum and dad? I asked the boy on the floor. Oh! This was Thorne as a little boy, I realised. And next to him baby Jack crawled about, a white bonnet on his head. Oh dear – that wasn't a good look!

"I don't see why you need a dog," the boy-Thorne said. "You never even seem to have time to play with *us* . . ."

No need to be jealous, Thorne, I told him. *Kids love dogs. And dogs love kids. You'll have a great time! You just have to learn how to speak Dog!*

"Now you're just being a silly-billy, aren't you?" said

Thorne's dad as he stroked the puppy. "Well? What have you got to say for yourself? Hmmmm?"

Boy-Thorne opened and closed his mouth without saying anything. Then: "Woof . . . "

"I think he's trying to say something." George's voice jolted me out of Thorne's dream.

I blinked, and looked around me. At least now I understood why Thorne was so weird around dogs. He was jealous! I almost felt sorry for him. But back in reality, Thorne lay on a stretcher in front of an ambulance. The Wilson family, Will, Jack and the workmen all crowded around him. "Woof," Thorne said.

I grinned at him. "See, you *can* speak Dog," I barked.

Thorne's eyes boggled at us all, as if he couldn't quite believe what was coming out of his mouth. "Woof . . . Woof, woof, woof!" he continued.

The crowd gasped in shock. Clearly, they all thought he'd finally lost it.

"Look after 'im," Jack said to the two paramedics as they wheeled him backwards into the ambulance. He patted Thorne's arm. "OK, we'll see yer soon."

"Pudsey, I made it!" came a voice.

Finn? I swung around. The old dog came galloping through the crowd.

"Oof, what's going on here? Have I missed anything?" he asked.

I was glad to see my friend. "Oh, not much. I just saved the day. Again." Well, a little bragging wouldn't hurt.

"Really? Oh, well done, Pudsey, ye mega-dog, ye."

"*Now* where are we going to live?" Tommy asked his mum as the paramedics slammed shut the back doors of the ambulance.

Jack turned to Gail. "There's always room at my place," he offered. "I mean, at least until the cottage is rebuilt . . . " He shrugged. "You know, if you want to."

"Aye, aye! Looks like ye'll be staying around then, Pudsey," said Finn.

"It looks like it! Come on, Gail," I barked. Was she ever going to answer Jack?

Gail looked at Tommy, George and Molly in turn, her eyebrows raised. They were all smiling.

"We'd love to," she told Jack with a nod as her cheeks flushed as pink as a flamingo.

Jack beamed. I'd never seen him smile properly before. And by the look of the sparkle in his eyes, he had a big soft spot for Gail. I was pretty sure she liked him too.

"Bingo!" Finn and I barked together. Did he think he was staying too, I wondered? I really wasn't sure there was room in this family for more than one dog – I didn't want to share them with anybody. They were much too special! I'd have to set Finn straight about that later.

We all watched on as the ambulance drove off, taking the woofing Thorne away from our home.

Good riddance, I thought.

"Can we go to the fete now?" asked Tommy.

"Of course!" Gail grinned. "With any luck, there will still be some cakes left!"

"I hope so," I barked. My belly rumbled like thunder at the mention of food. Now that I'd saved the day, my appetite had well and truly returned! I was so glad to see everyone reunited and safe. *Pie and gravy . . . pie and gravy . . . pie and gravy . . . Mmmmmmm.*

CHAPTER TWENTY-THREE

We left Gail's car at the farm and all rode in Jack's truck to the fete. I sat on Gail's lap in the passenger seat, grinning from ear to ear as she stroked my ears. I'd saved the farm. I'd really done it. I really was Pudsey the mega-dog (not that I'd ever been in any doubt about that, of course).

The first thing I saw as Jack parked the car next to the village green was some children skipping around a maypole, the multi-coloured ribbons weaving round and round. So they *did* do that in the countryside! We all leapt out of the truck. *Pie and gravy . . . pie and gravy* ... the words ran around in my head. On the stage, some men in white trousers, black blazers and red braces danced about. They had bells on their shoes which jingled like tambourines. And they waved white handkerchiefs in both hands as they skipped back and forth. It was all very strange, but several villagers were watching their show and clapping in time to the accordion music. I made a mental note to look up that kind of dancing online later – that's if the cottage ever got WiFi. I could teach them a thing or two about how to strut their stuff, I thought. Hadn't they ever heard of street-dance?

I ran around the fete, my nose firmly in smell-o-tron mode (as George called it). *Pie and gravy ... pie and gravy* ... Where was Peter's pie stall? *Oh, I hope he's hasn't thrown it all away after the spilled pie disaster!*

Finally I found the stall where a grim-faced Peter

stood behind the giant pie. He was sticking his finger into the gravy and frowning. It had survived! Well, some of it, at least! The golden pastry lid was nowhere to be seen, but I sniffed in a deep delicious waft of beef in succulent gravy. *Mmmmmmmmmm ... pie ...*

I crept up towards it, staying low on all fours. Plan A: I was hoping there'd be chunks and crumbs on the floor from the spillage that I could hoover up before Peter noticed.

I reached the table and began snuffling in the grass. I found a couple of pastry flakes which I gobbled up with gusto, but otherwise there was nothing! I put my paws to my stomach as it gave a tremendous belly-rumble. *Uh-oh.* I hoped Peter hadn't heard it over the accordion music.

"Who's that there?"

I curled into a ball. Perhaps I was hidden under the tablecloth.

"Pudsey? What are you doing 'ere?"

I shuffled out from under the table, emerging at Peter's side. *Time for Plan B*, I thought. I had nothing to lose!

I stood up on my hind legs and bent my paws in the begging position. "Please, sir," I barked, "can I have some pie?" (Yes, you're right, I stole that line from *Oliver*.)

Peter waggled his finger at me ... and then grinned. "Well, I 'aven't won the prize now, 'ave I? You might as well 'ave it all, Pudsey – better than me chucking it in the bin!"

"Really? All of it?" I could hardly believe my floppy ears.

In answer, Peter wrapped his arms around the pie, heaved it from the table and nestled it down on the grass next to me. I gulped in awesome anticipation of what was to follow. "Thank ... mmm ... 'ou ... Peter ... mmmm," I barked as I began savouring every mouthful of the rich, beefy gravy. I'd eat that first, then the beef chunks, then the buttery golden pastry. (I always recommend having a clear strategy to food eating – it makes it *so* much more pleasurable.)

By the time I'd eaten the last morsel of pie, my stomach bulged with satisfaction. *No running around until this has gone down,* I told myself. No dog likes to get indigestion!

I walked back past the stalls. "Pudsey, look at this!" It was George's voice. I stopped and turned around – and saw George with a hammer next to the strong-man meter. Behind him was a group of girls, all giggling. It looked like George had a few admirers – and he seemed to be enjoying the attention!

"Now, are you ready to see the strongest man in all of Chuffington?" he asked his crowd. "Let me intro-duce you to George – the Great Muscleman – Wilson!"

He heaved the hammer behind his shoulder,

sucked in a deep breath through his nostrils, then swung the hammer down with a grunt.

Bing!!!!!! rang the golden bell at the top of the meter.

"Oh, well done, George!" I barked as he bowed to the girls. I suddenly had a thought: I hoped these girls didn't all start hanging around the house! I knew what soppy-eyed tweens were like when they thought they were in love. (You won't be surprised to know I've had a fair few admirers hanging around me in the past. My top tip to get rid of a love-struck dog? Chew on a chicken foot with your mouth open. Works every time.)

As the girls continued gazing at George, I skipped away. (I could feel the pie being slowly digested now – I'd be ready for seconds soon. *I'd better keep my smell-o-tron – aka my nose – on high alert . . .*)

Oh, look, there's Tommy! He leant over the circular hook-a-duck stall with a rod, dangling it above a little pond where yellow ducks floated about (I was relieved to see they were fake – I don't condone cruelty to any animal, even quacky ducks).

"Come on!" he said to himself as he tried to hook one of the plastic ducks with his rod.

"Go on, Tommy, you can do it!" I said encouragingly, coming up alongside him and resting my paws on the ledge to watch.

Tommy steadied the rod above the pond and then ... "Gotcha!" he yelled.

The lady who owned the stall smiled, lifted the duck up and stared at its bottom.

That's a bit rude! I thought. *Even if it isn't real!*

"Oh, you've won our special prize," she told Tommy. "Well done!"

Ah, so they have the prizes written on their backsides. Well, you learn something new every day.

The lady grabbed a giant fluffy tiger that had been hanging on a stall post.

Tommy beamed as she passed it to him. I groaned – aren't tigers just big stripy cats?! Then I sighed – well, at least this one wasn't real. But where were the toy dogs, I ask you? There seemed to be a distinct lack of them around here. I'd have to change that.

"I'm going to call it Thomas," Tommy told me as he tucked the tiger under his arm, looking the happiest I'd ever seen him. I couldn't begrudge him that.

We walked to the stage together, passing a prancing George on the way. He waved white handkerchiefs in both hands, dancing around like a lizard who'd had too many ants for breakfast. "I'm a Morris dancer!" he told us. "Look!"

So *that's* what they were called. "Don't hurt yourself, George! Stick to the strongman career!" I barked. He might have been an ace gamer, and could throw a hammer like a pro, but as for dancing? He had a long way to go if he had any hope of being the next Justin Timberlake!

On the stage, the Morris dancers still waved their handkerchiefs up and down. (*I hope they're clean*, I suddenly thought. I mean, I like mud and dirt as much as the next dog, but slimy green human bogeys? They're just gross.) On the grass in front of the stage, Will and Molly spun around, arm in arm. If I thought I had a smile on my face after all that pie, it couldn't have been half as big as the beams on both of theirs, stretching from ear to ear.

I scampered up to Gail, who stood watching Molly and Will, nodding her head to the music. Jack came up and tapped Gail on the shoulder.

"Madam, can I 'ave the pleasure of this dance?" he asked in a fake posh accent. Ha ha – he'd never sound like his brother, even if he tried! Nonetheless, it made me think of Thorne. I hoped he was OK – really I did. He had looked pretty out of it as he left in the ambulance. Anyway, now that his plans to destroy the farm were ruined, I thought that maybe he'd come to his senses – especially with me around to show him how awesome the family were, including me, a dog! I was certain I could change his mind about our species.

Gail's cheeks flushed pink and she smiled at Jack. "Why yes, kind sir," she replied with a curtsey. Jack took Gail's hand and pulled her towards the rest of the dancing villagers.

As they began twirling about, I sniffed the air. I could smell something sweet ... something fried ... something *delicious. Ah, there!* Molly sat on a hay bale with her legs dangling down, and Will was walking up to her holding out a greasy paper bag. *Time to get cute and irresistible!* I thought, as I stood up on hind legs and did the quick-step over to the two love-birds.

"Hey, Molly," I barked as I skipped from side to

side. "What's that you've got there?" (Sometimes I find the sweet and innocent approach works best.)

Molly looked up, winked at me and held out the bag. "Come on then, Pudsey. After saving Tommy – and the farm – you probably deserve a hundred of these!"

A hundred? I am SO going to keep her to that. And I didn't even have to beg! "You heard her, didn't you, Will?" I barked.

He laughed and stroked my head as I munched on the soft fluffy donut. *I am in heaven,* I thought.

As I licked the sugary crumbs around my mouth, I looked out at the fete-goers. There was George at the coconut shy, punching the air as he hit the targets one by one, the girls still giggling behind him. Gail and Jack were pulling Tommy over to dance, all three laughing as they skipped around in a circle. Then there was Molly and Will on the hay

221

bales holding hands, their cheeks pink with young love. *Aaaahhhh* ... I told you I was a softy deep down!

It was obvious that the family – *my* family – were well and truly part of the village now. Including me! *We're here to stay*, I told myself as Will dropped another donut into my paws. I grinned. *And I'm not going to complain about that.*

"Don't worry," I sang to myself, suddenly remembering the song the busker in London had played, "be happy." Except that now I'd made up some new lyrics. "In my life I've got a new family, humans to care about – people who love me. Oh, don't worry, be happy!" I swallowed the donut in one gulp, then jumped off the hay bales and skipped over to Nelly, Edward, Ken and Finn, who I'd spotted at the edge of the fete in the petting corner.

"Oh, Edward, look at those two!" Nelly was saying, nodding in the direction of two sleek black shire horses pulling a carriage around the village green. "They're *gorgeous*."

Eddie raised his eyebrows. "Why are you always looking at other men, Nelly?" he complained. "Are you unhappy at home?"

Nelly sighed. "No, Edward. They're just ... well ... hot-to-trot!"

I scampered along to Finn, who was rolling around on the grass while a toddler and his dad tickled Finn's tummy.

"Aye, aye, Pudsey!" said Finn. "This fete is super, so it is!"

"It's *paw*some, isn't it?" I laughed as the toddler tickled Finn's chin and he let out a loud Scottish giggle.

"Aye, I wish I could stay, I really do – but I'm gonna have te rush off soon."

"Oh, really?" I asked. Secretly I was relieved – even though I liked Finn, I couldn't bear the thought of sharing the Wilsons with him – but I didn't let it show.

"Aye – I've got to catch the next train to London. Planning to try me hand at busking – I figure I cannae keep this voice from entertaining the world!"

I grinned. "You should start with Piccadilly Circus," I told him. "It's one of my favourite spots!"

I skipped to the very end of the petting area, where Ken wandered around a pen. I blinked. Was that a blown-up rubber glove on his head ... and a feather-covered blanket around his body? Now he was *dressed* like a chicken. Had he lost it completely?

I jumped up and put my front paws on the fence so I could chat to him. "Hi, Ken!" I barked.

"It's *hen*!" he grunted.

"Oh ... right ... Erm, nice hat!"

"Thanks," he replied in his deep, piggy, not-at-all-like-a-chicken voice.

"Isn't this great?" I said to him, pointing at all the happy people dancing behind us.

"Oh yeah. But I've got somefink even *better*."

I was confused – what did he mean? "Better than your *hat*?"

He beckoned to me with a piggy hoof. "Get in 'ere 'n' 'ave a butchers."

"Um, OK . . . ?" I hurdled the fence.

Once I was in, Ken pointed to something in the corner.

"Wow, Ken!" I cried. Nestled on a pile of hay was not, as I'd expected, a dollop of steaming pig poo – but a perfect, cream-coloured egg. I couldn't believe my eyes. Maybe he hadn't lost it after all . . . "Ken! You finally did it!"

"Ha, ha, ha," Ken chuckled. "I said I could!"

We both stared at the egg some more. I blinked, and blinked again. Yep – it was still there!

"Well I never," I barked. Then my stomach

rumbled. *Hhhhmm, wait a minute. A pig? Laying eggs? That makes bacon and eggs – all rolled into one! Eggs and bacon . . . eggs and bacon . . .*

I turned to Ken, my brain buzzing like a bee doing overtime. "With this invention," I told him as I clapped my paws together in glee, "we'll be rich!"

I took one last look around the village green. My new friends and new family, all together, everyone happy. All because of me! Well, partly because of me. *I could definitely like it here*, I told myself. It's not a bad place for a dog to live – even a city dog like me.

PAWS FOR THOUGHT – AN INTERVIEW WITH PUDSEY

Hi there, Pudsey fans! I'm delighted to say we've been granted an interview with Pudsey, just after the final take. Come and take a look inside his shiny silver trailer. Can you see him? There's Pudsey, reclining on a black leather sofa, a plate of sausages on the table next to him. This is so exciting! Are you ready for an exclusive, readers?

Pudsey: Please, come in and take a seat. Let me just turn off this episode of *Lassie* ... It's the one where Lassie takes part in a dog show. It's my favourite!

Interviewer: So Pudsey, this is your silver screen debut, right?

Pudsey: Yes, it's my first film – but that didn't stop me becoming a pro at the acting thing right away. The director said I was a natural. Woof!

Interviewer: Did you enjoy making the film?

Pudsey: Absolutely – it was a blast! Especially the food scenes – eating a giant pie from the inside out really was a dream come true. Can you imagine all the juicy, rich gravy and huge meaty chunks of beef? *Mmmmmmmmmm* ... [Note: at this point Pudsey's eyes glaze over.]

Interviewer: Um, Pudsey?

Pudsey: Sorry, yes, where was I? The pie! It was a good job I had all the running to do in the later scenes to work it off though. Got to keep this physique in trim, you know!

Interviewer: How does the off-screen Pudsey differ from the on-screen one?

Pudsey: Not much, to be honest! It's true that my favourite thing is food, followed by chasing pigeons, followed by being chased. Although I should say that my favourite type of sausage is venison, not Cumberland – just in case any fans want to send me a gift or anything ... Oh, and I don't think I'd ever put up with sleeping in a doggy prison or barn. That straw really is super-itchy!

Interviewer: What were the humans like to work with? Did they all give you treats?

Pudsey: The kids were lovely – even the bully-boy. He's actually a big softy in real life. He gave me a dog biscuit every time we did a scene together. And Molly is hilarious – she kept pulling funny faces before takes, which had me in stitches, especially when she was wearing that silly blue hat! I had to bite on a bone just to calm down. But the leading lady was a *nightmare* – she kept sneezing when I was around, refused to touch me, and didn't give me one treat! She won't read this, right? I was SO relieved I only had one scene with her.

Interviewer: There are some particularly nail-biting moments in the film, like when you almost get hit by the van and when you save Tommy in front of the digger. Do you do your own stunts, or do you have a stunt double?

Pudsey (puffing his chest out): I do all my stunts myself! I really am an incredible gymnast, you know, and I'm not scared of a bit of hard work. They wouldn't have been able to get a stunt double as talented as me, anyway. And I wanted the movie to be as authentic as possible. I really can do all of those things!

Interviewer: The dance scene in the doggy prison is one of my favourites. How long did it take you to learn the routine?

Pudsey: I love that scene too. Dancing is my fourth best thing! As I'm sure you know, I was already a professional dancer, so I actually choreographed that whole scene myself. I practised for a couple of hours before filming, and we did it in one take! The dogs really were completely mesmerised – and Simon made me promise to teach it to him!

Interviewer: This trailer is awesome. Do you have any particular requests for things whilst on location?

Pudsey: Thanks! I designed it myself. And I'm pretty easy to please – all I ask for is a constant supply of venison sausages . . . And not to be woken up before 9 am!

Interviewer: So, Pudsey, all the girls want to know: is there any special lady-dog in your life right now?

Pudsey grins and his cheeks flush: No, not right now. You know, I'm pretty happy being single. I'm not quite ready to share my sausages with anyone else. But I wouldn't count it out later on in life . . .

Interviewer: Did you hear that, readers? Watch this space . . . Finally, Pudsey, we have to ask: What's Ken like in real life? Does he really think he's a chicken?

Pudsey: Ha ha – no, not really. You know he hated having to wear that blown-up rubber glove on his head so much, I hid it in his bed for a joke! But he's a good sport, really – we had a lot of fun filming those 'I'm a chicken' scenes. He's hoping for his own eggs and bacon movie now, of course!

Thank you so much, Pudsey. A legend in your own lifetime, we salute you!

ACKNOWLEDGEMENTS

All great actors need a team behind them. And when you're also a world-famous dancing dog with four legs, a tail and a permanent coat, you need a top-notch team – the very best.

Firstly, I must thank Ashleigh Butler. Without Ashleigh, the book and film wouldn't exist, because – and I will let you in on a secret here – I only know what to do when Ashleigh tells me. Thanks also to Grandma Penny and Grandpa Ian (who look after Ashleigh) and to Aunt Tayla and Uncle Brett, who really should be thanking me – after all, they get to live with the world's most talented dog.

Like Brad Pitt, Leonardo DiCaprio and George Clooney, all great actors need a manager. I have not one, but two! Thank you to Professor Jonathan Shalit, my manager and an executive producer of my film, and Lucy Marriott (previously Nazli Alizadeh), at ROAR Global, London.

I have a personal director and producers too, of course – Nick Moore, Rupert Preston and Marshall Leviten. Thank you, guys. You gave me my dream – and I don't mean starring in my own film (although that is pretty awesome). You kept your promise and gave me unlimited venison sausages. *Mmmm, sausages . . .*

Thanks to Catherine Coe, who helped me write this book. That's another secret! But there was no way I was tiring out my delicate paws by typing all these words! And not forgetting Paul Rose, who Professor

Jonathan introduced me to in order to write – under my expert eye – the script for the film.

Lassie used to be the most famous dog in the world. He made eleven movies. Then I came along and won *Britain's Got Talent* – and I'm going to make fifteen. This is only the beginning.

Love,

Pudsey